A WHOLE NEW ANGLE

"Shut up, Matt. I like this guy. He's cool. Don't you dare mention tutoring me in geometry. Just be quiet." I broke into a smile. "Hi, Zach."

Zach nodded at me, then eyed Matt. "Who are you?"

Matt hesitated for a sec, then he threw his arm around my shoulder and hauled me up against him. "Natalie's boyfriend."

What? I whirled around to confront him, but the second I was facing him, he grabbed me by the shoulders and kissed me. Then he released me and flipped me a grin. "See you tonight, darlin'."

Smart Boys & Fast Girls

STEPHIE DAVIS

SMOOCH NEW YORK CITY

SMOOCH ®

September 2005

Published by

Dorchester Publishing Co., Inc.
200 Madison Avenue
New York, NY 10016

ISBN 0-8439-5398-5

Visit us on the web at www.smoochya.com.

My sincerest appreciation to my technical consultants on cross-country running: Rowe the Evangelist and Elyse Kopecky, who read my book in one day to meet my deadline. You guys rock! Any cross-country errors are mine and mine alone.

Thank you to my wonderful and supportive agent, Michelle Grajkowski, who makes me laugh late at night with her goofy emails. TK forever!

Thanks also to my fabulous editor, Kate Seaver, for all your support. And thanks to Leah Hultenschmidt and the rest of the Dorchester staff for all your hard work on my behalf.

And thanks to my mom, for being the best PR manager on the planet!

Smart Boys
&
Fast Girls

1

The first thing I noticed about the varsity cross-country team was that the boys were way cuter than they were on junior varsity. And taller. And had deeper voices. And were way more interested in girls than the JV boys.

Unfortunately, I wasn't one of the girls earning all the attention.

Nope. I was sitting on the bottom bench of the metal bleachers stretching my hamstrings, watching the older girls laugh and flirt with the very cute older guys. We'd been having practice for almost six weeks already, and I still couldn't get the guys to look my way when the urge to flirt came across them.

Story of my life.

My name is Natalie Page and there are several things you should know about me.

First, I'm a sophomore at Mapleville High. Running is my life, and I made varsity this year. I'm so excited! Too bad I don't know anyone on the team and I feel like I have the plague or something when I'm at practice. Why aren't the girls more friendly?

Second, I have three awesome best friends named Blue Waller, Allie Morrison and Frances Spinelli. Unfortunately, all three of them have boyfriends, leaving me the odd one out. A major problem when it comes to Friday and Saturday nights, and it makes the lack of bonding with the varsity girls even more of a problem. I miss my JV friends—not that I'd trade varsity for some Friday night plans.

Third, it's time for me to have a boyfriend. Unfortunately, I'm one of those girls that has tons of guy pals (mostly runners from my team—and that was last year on JV; the varsity boys haven't even noticed me as a buddy yet!) and no boyfriends. Boys love me as a buddy, a pal, someone to push into a mud puddle on a rainy run, knowing they'll get it right back. I know more guys than any of my friends, but I'm the only one going solo to the first school dance of the year—if I go. I mean, do I really want to go alone?

Fourth, the boy I have fallen madly in love with is Zach Fulton. He has this really dark hair that curls at the back of his neck the tiniest little bit. It's always a little messy-looking, and soooo cute! His eyes are a deep brown that make my stomach go all wiggly, and he has this truly gorgeous smile. He's the captain of the boys' team, and every other girl on the squad is in love with him, too. Which means I'm never going to be able to get his attention.

So anyway, that's me. Nothing too exciting, huh? Just Natalie the loser.

"So, um, Nat. We need to talk." I looked up as Allie

dropped to the bench next to me. She was wearing a cropped shirt and a black mini that looked awesome on her.

For a moment, I felt totally ugly next to her. I hated it when I let her do that to me. It wasn't like she did it on purpose. "What's up, Allie?"

"About Friday night . . ."

"I'm totally pumped!" Friday was going to be girls' night. It was down to only once a month since my friends all had boyfriends, but they'd all agreed to forego their dudes for me this Friday, and I was psyched! We were going to the mall for dinner and shopping, then a late movie. "We're going to have the best time and I got this new shirt and—"

"We're going to have to bag on you."

My gut sank. "What? Why?"

"Well, I'm not going to see Tad all week, so I'll be totally missing him, and Blue got tickets to a play that Colin's been wanting to see and Frances wants to go down to Harvard Square and hang out with Theo. You don't mind, do you?"

I bit my lip and tried to ignore the tightening of my throat. "No, that's fine." Sure, I didn't mind sitting at home *again* while they were all out with the boyfriends. So the four of us had been best friends since we could walk. Obviously that didn't matter once boys got into the picture. I sighed. This *sucked*.

"You sure you're not mad?"

"It's *fine*." I blinked harder. Totally stupid to cry just because my friends didn't need me in their lives anymore.

"I knew you'd understand."

"Yeah, sure." *I understand.* Who needs to hang with their single friend when you could swap spit with a guy? If only I had some other life to fill in for them ditching me. Unfortunately, there was nada.

Allie elbowed me. "So, now that we got that out of the way, I have to ask: Who's the guy in the red T-shirt? He's delish."

I didn't even need to look. I knew exactly who was wearing the red T-shirt today. "That's Zach Fulton. Team captain."

"Yum. If I wasn't already taken, I'd be following him back to the locker room."

Oh, so she needed two boyfriends to my none?

"Tell me about it." I switched legs and leaned forward.

"Aha. Do I detect a little interest from Natalie, Miss I Never Date Runners?"

"Just because I noticed he's cute doesn't mean I want to date him." I watched him flip the ponytail of a tall blonde. Valerie is a senior, the best runner on the girls' team, and our captain. "Though for him, I might make an exception."

"I guess that means practice is going better?"

I sighed. My friends didn't love me, and I was ostracized at practice. Life was grand. "Not really. The team is like a really tight clique with no room for anyone else. The girls won't talk to me, and Zach doesn't know I'm alive." With my friends all drooling over their boyfriends, I was in dire need of some other people to hang out with. Either that or I was going to become the biggest loser in the school. We're talking zero social life.

"Hey, Natalie!"

I turned around so fast I lost my balance and almost fell off the bench and onto my face. Valerie was smiling at me. "Great job in the race on Sunday."

Oh, wow. "Thanks."

"Who was that?" Allie nudged me.

"Oh my God. She's the number-one girl on our team, and she's the captain. Do you realize she just spoke to me?"

Another girl named Marcie nodded at me as she walked onto the field. "Nice race, Nat."

I managed to stutter out another thanks and I grabbed the bench to steady myself. "Oh my God. Did you see that?"

"How'd you do in the race?" Allie asked. "Must have been good."

"I scored second for our team. We won the meet by two points." Was that it? Because I'd helped them win, I was in? It was the first race I'd run well in this year. All the others I'd been too nervous, but last weekend, I'd been particularly cranky because my friends had all ditched me again, so I'd just gone out and run hard, not worrying about anything else. And it had worked.

Zach leaned over and whispered something to Valerie, and then nodded at me.

I clutched Allie's leg. "Zach noticed me!"

"I saw." She peeled my fingers off of her thigh.

"Why don't you get off this bench and go out there and stretch with the rest of the team? Find a spot next to Zach."

"I couldn't do that." My hand went to my hair to make sure my ponytail wasn't lumpy. "I tried to stretch with them the first day, and they all got up and moved. It was so embarrassing."

Valerie waved at me again. "Come down here, Natalie. Stretch with us."

I nearly squealed, but Allie smacked me in the side with her elbow. "Be cool," she hissed.

Right. Be cool. I let my breath out, shook out my shoulders, and rose casually to my feet. "Sure." And then I sauntered slowly across the field, waiting for someone to yell "April Fool's" and have everyone jump up and take off across the grass.

But no one moved, and Valerie patted the ground next to her.

Next to Valerie? I could get a spot next to Valerie? That was totally the sign that I'd been accepted. She ruled the team, and if she said people were in or out, then they were.

I sat down next to her and held my breath.

"You know, if you keep running like you did this weekend, we have a chance to win state," Valerie said. "We needed a good fifth runner, and instead, we got a second runner. Keep it up, Natalie."

Oh my gosh. This was incredible. Valerie thought I was cool! "I'll do my best," I said.

Valerie's gaze narrowed slightly. "As long as your best is good enough."

Crud. "It will be."

"Good." She nodded at the other girls sitting around with us. "Natalie will run with us today."

With them? I was going to run with them? I mean, we all ran together, but the team always ended up spread out in bunches. I'd tried to run with Valerie's group the first week, but they'd literally stopped running every time I came near. Well, that wasn't totally true. The first couple times they sped up and tried to lose me. When they couldn't, they just stopped.

So I ran with the slower girls in the back.

But now I could run with Valerie? And her friends?

I bent my face over my knee and tried not to look too pathetically grateful. I was a sophomore. Totally worthy of hanging with seniors, right?

What if she invited me to a party? A party with Zach?

My breath caught in my throat and I started coughing.

The real number-two girl, who had come in behind me this weekend, pounded on my back. "You okay, sophomore girl? Can't have you hacking up your lungs until the season's over."

Oh my gosh. I was in. I was in!

All I had to do was keep running fast. Not a problem if I was going to be allowed to train with them. They'd make me faster. And then they'd like me more. And then maybe Zach would notice me. And then I'd have a social life, and it wouldn't matter that my friends all had boyfriends. I'd have one too, and I'd go to parties and I'd be cool. No more Natalie with three friends who had all abandoned her. No more Natalie who no boys ever noticed except as a buddy.

Thanks to my legs, my life had just changed. My sophomore year had gone from Friday nights with the television and runs all by myself to "in" with Valerie and her friends, one of whom was Zach. Sure, it was a perk that would probably disappear if I started blowing up at meets, but I wasn't about to let that happen.

No way.

Me and my running shoes were going to kick butt for the rest of the season, and my social life was going to be the benefactor.

"Natalie! Can you come over here?" Coach Thompson was standing away from the group, his clipboard in his hand.

I jumped to my feet and sprinted over. Gotta look fast all the time so they don't change their minds. "What's up, Coach?"

"I got a call from Ms. Olsen just now."

My math teacher? "What did she want?"

"To remove you from the team."

I blinked. "What?"

"Natalie, you've failed all three geometry tests this year."

"Yeah, but—" My heart started racing and I felt sweat between my shoulder blades.

"No buts, Natalie. You have to get that grade up or you're off the team for rest of the season."

Off the team? But the team was my life. It was everything, and I'd just made it over the hump. I couldn't walk away now! Tears burned in the back of my eyes, and I bit my lip to keep from crying. I would *not* cry in front of Coach. "I'll do better, I promise."

He nodded, then seemed to hesitate. After a moment, he said, "Listen, Natalie, you have the talent to be number one on this team."

No way? Really? My heart did a triple flip and I wanted to scream. Not only would I be in Valerie's inner circle, but I'd also be the best runner? Oh my gosh!

"But if you end up sitting for this entire season, it's really going to affect your chances."

If I had to miss the season, I'd be out. Out before I was even in. "I'm not going to sit." No way. "I'll get my geometry grade up. I'll turn it into an A." I couldn't lose this opportunity because of stupid geometry!

"Good." He slapped my shoulder. "That's what I wanted to hear. We're going to need you this season. I told Ms. Olsen you'd be right over to meet your new tutor."

"My tutor?" Was he kidding? "I don't need a tutor."

"It's the tutor or no team."

If my parents found out I'd been assigned a tutor, they'd make me drop running in a heartbeat. Running was fine only if it didn't interfere with my grades. I had to pass geometry on my own. I *was* going to get an A. I had to! But a tutor was out of the question. "Can't I just promise to study? I have a smart friend who goes to another school. She can help me."

"Tutor or no team. Your pick."

This sucked. I mean, it really sucked. Everyone made fun of the kids who needed tutors, because you had to be pretty stupid to need a tutor. Imagine if the team found out? It didn't matter how fast I ran, I'd be out. No Valerie, no Zach, no friends. No way!

So what if I was having a little trouble with geometry? Who wouldn't? With all those dumb proofs and angles and whatever. It made no sense. It didn't mean I was stupid!

"Aren't there any other options besides a tutor?" There had to be.

He shook his head. "Meet with Ms. Olsen now and convince her that you'll work harder in geometry. If you don't, she'll file a recommendation with the principal to take you off the team for at least this semester."

Which would be for the entire cross-country season. I'd miss the whole season, and I'd be labeled stupid and everything would suck. Tears surged again, and this time I couldn't stop them. So I turned away from Coach and pretended to tie my shoe.

Coach Thompson pointed toward the school. "If you hustle, maybe you can make it back for the end of practice."

"Now? I have to go now?" But I was going to get to run in Valerie's group.

"Maybe missing practice today will help you to realize the seriousness of the situation, what you stand to lose."

"I know what I'll lose." What kind of stupid remark

was that? As if I needed a lesson on the importance of cross country.

"Then go."

I was going. But not to sign up with a tutor. I had to talk Ms. Olsen out of this ridiculous idea. Maybe I could convince her to let me drop her class. Yes, that's what I'd do. Blue said her sister had already dropped a class in college because it was too hard. Why couldn't I do it here? I'd drop the class, keep my grades up and I'd be able to run.

"Where are you going?" Allie grabbed my arm as I ran past her. "Aren't you going to practice?"

"I have to do an errand for Coach." I pulled my arm free and sprinted away before she could question me. See why I had to change Ms. Olsen's mind? Because people were going to notice something was up.

No way could I lose running, and no way was I stupid enough to need a tutor. I *had* to solve this problem *now.* And I had to solve it fast so I could get back before practice was over. I couldn't miss my chance to become friends with Valerie, to actually be accepted by the other girls on the team.

I ran all the way to Ms. Olsen's classroom, taking the stairs three at a time, courtesy of my abnormally long legs. I know long legs sound good, but mine are at least two feet longer than my upper body. Good for running, but bad for everything else, like trying to look normal or find clothes that fit.

Stephie Davis

Ms. Olsen was sitting at her desk when I jumped through her doorway. "Ms. Olsen. I'm here."

She glanced up, then checked her watch. "Already?"

"Yes." I wiped sweat off my forehead and waited for my breath to catch up with me. "Coach told me that you called him, and I wanted to talk to you."

"Apparently." She gestured to a seat. "It's about your grades."

"Yeah, I know." I sat where she'd told me, trying to play the role of the dedicated student. "But I've started studying with my friend Frances, who's a straight-A student at North Valley School for Girls. She's going to help me."

She arched her brow. "When did you start studying with her?"

"Um . . ." Given that the last test I failed was this morning, it didn't give me much maneuvering room. "We start tonight."

Her fingers drummed on the desk. So annoying. "That's fine if you want to study with your friend, but you also have to work with the tutor I assign."

I tried not to grimace. "But Ms. Olsen, I don't need a tutor."

"You've failed every test and your homework assignments are a disaster."

"Yeah, but . . ."

"Natalie. School is more important than sports, and I am not one of those teachers who will make exceptions for athletes. I called Coach Thompson out of courtesy to tell him I was recommending that you be taken off the team, but he convinced me to try the tutor route."

So it was Coach's fault I was going to be stuck with a tutor? "Ms. Olsen, please give me another chance to prove I can do better on my own. I really don't need a tutor. I'll work harder. I promise." She never would have kicked me off the team. It had just been a threat, and now Coach had given her this tutor idea.

She picked up a piece of paper and handed it to me.

It was a memo from her to our principal, signed and dated today. The recommendation to boot me from the team was more like a command than a request, and no principal was going to turn it down. Tension clamped in my stomach. "You're not going to send this, are you?"

"It will sit in my top drawer. One more grade below a B minus and I'm sending it."

I had to get a B minus? There was no way I could get a B minus on my own. Maybe, just maybe, I could avoid failing if Frances helped me, but a B minus?

"If you don't average Bs the rest of the semester, you won't be able to pull your grades up enough to pass the course. Bs or you're off the team. And I will be grading your homework as well, so that better be good too."

My homework, too? I swallowed and tried not to panic. "Please, you can't take the team away from me."

"I sure can." She handed me another piece of paper. "Your tutor's name is Matt Turner. I already spoke to him. He's expecting your call and is ready to start tonight for the homework assignment due tomorrow."

She looked at her watch. "He said he'd be in the library until four o'clock, so you can catch him if you hurry."

As if I was going to race to the library so I could meet my tutor in public! Everyone was going to think I was such a loser if they found out I had a tutor. I wasn't cool enough to withstand that kind of hit to my reputation. Now I was merely a social oversight. If word got out that I was so stupid I needed a tutor, then I'd be an out-cast. Fat chance of that. "I have to go back to practice."

Her eyes narrowed and she suddenly looked like a psycho-killer teacher. "You want me to send the memo now?"

"No!"

"Then convince me that you're going to take geometry seriously."

"I'm going to!" I hated teachers. Hated them! How could she take away the one thing that mattered to me? Because of stupid geometry! Her ego was way too big if she thought geometry was more important to my future than running. Who got college scholarships from geometry, huh? Running was my ticket to higher education. And she wanted to pull me off the team?

No way. I would show her I didn't need a dumb tutor. "Is that all?" I clutched the paper with Matt's name and number and tried to keep my voice calm.

"This is for your own good, Natalie. Someday you'll thank me."

Yeah, right. There was zero chance of that.

I stood up and walked to the door. If I turned right,

that would take me back to practice. Left took me to the library.

Her beady eyes were boring into my back, so I turned left. When I reached the end of the hall, I glanced back. She was standing in her doorway watching me.

What? Didn't she trust me? So now I was stupid *and* a liar?

Great. This day was going great.

I could have been hanging with Zach and Valerie. Instead, I was going to meet a tutor.

He'd better not make fun of me or I would be so out of there.

2

I was surprised at how busy the library was. I'd had no idea this many kids were there after school. I never thought about what people who weren't at practice did. It was a whole other world, I guess.

As if I was supposed to be able to find Matt Turner here. I didn't even know what he looked like.

"Natalie! Over here!"

I spun to my right to see a geek from my geometry class waving at me. *Please don't tell me that's Matt.* It was bad enough to have a tutor, but I figured he'd at least be a junior or a senior. To have someone in my own class be so much smarter than me was the ultimate humiliation.

Maybe it's not Matt. Maybe Matt asked him to look out for me and he's going to direct me to where Matt is. Yes, that's it.

I sidled over to his table. "Yes?"

"You didn't bring your books."

"Yeah, I got called out of cross-country practice." I

tried to catch a peek at his notebook to see whether his name was on it. No luck.

"You talked to Ms. Olsen?"

"Uh-huh." I might as well ask, I guess. "Are you Matt Turner?"

If I wasn't mistaken, he looked completely offended for a split second, then a cool mask dropped over his face. "You don't even know my name? We're in the same class."

"Yeah, I know. I recognize you from geometry." I wasn't a snob, I swear. It's just that I didn't spend a lot of time paying close attention in Ms. Olsen's class. She was the most boring, worst teacher ever . . . wait a sec. That's why I was failing. Because she was a bad teacher. Not because I was stupid!

Then I frowned. So how come Matt could learn from her? Nice try, Nat, but apparently, you really are stupid. "So, are you Matt?"

He nodded once, his face still cold.

"Oh, come on, Matt. Don't take offense. So I don't know your name. There's a lot of people's names I don't know."

"Yeah, everyone who you don't think is worthy."

I frowned. "What kind of comment is that? I'm not a snob." Far from it. I was basically a loser, remember?

"I could care less." He gestured to the book. "I'm being paid to improve your grade, so that's what I'm here for."

"They're paying you?"

He nodded and looked a little smug. Or maybe it was

my total insecurity with the situation reading things into it. "Seven bucks an hour."

"You're kidding." I felt like collapsing into the nearest chair. I was so stupid they had to pay someone seven bucks an hour to make me smart?

Maybe I was wrong. Maybe running wasn't the key to my future. Maybe I needed to become a tutor.

Yeah, as if that was an option. Obviously, you couldn't tutor if you were dumb. So that left me with running. Which was fine. I loved it. So there.

"They're paying me extra for you."

I blinked. "Because I'm so hopeless?" *Don't cry. Don't cry. Don't cry.*

A flicker of emotion crossed his face. Sympathy? Because he knew how pathetic I was? I blinked harder to keep the tears at bay.

"Because it's such a big-time commitment. We have to meet every night to do your homework, and then plan extra sessions on the weekends to catch you up," he said.

I slumped. "Six days a week?"

"What? You can't bear to be with me that often?" He laughed. "Sorry, Natalie, but you're stuck with me." He seemed extremely amused by that fact.

"Why are you laughing?" He was laughing at me, wasn't he? Because he couldn't believe anyone was as stupid as I was. Great. This was *great*.

"Because it's funny to see you pouting. Sports only take you so far in this world."

I wanted to make a snide remark about the uselessness of brains, but I couldn't exactly do that, could I? We both knew brains were a good thing. I wondered how long he was going to make me pay for the fact that I hadn't known his name. Not that I didn't deserve his treatment, because I knew what it felt like to be overlooked.

Oh, super. Thanks to Matt, I now felt stupid *and* like a mean jerk. I felt totally guilty for not knowing his name and making him feel bad, because I knew how much it sucked not to be worthy of notice. I experienced it every day at cross-country practice.

Until today. Today things had changed. I had a chance to be cool. But only if I got back there before the window of opportunity closed. "As you can see, I don't have my stuff for math at the moment." I looked at my watch. Almost four. Shoot. Practice would be over soon. "What's your schedule later on?"

He sat back in his chair and hooked his hands behind his head. If it weren't for those glasses and the smug look on his face, he might even be cute. I sort of liked his short haircut, and even his clothes weren't that bad. I mean, they weren't *cool*, but they weren't so embarrassing that I couldn't be seen in the same stratosphere as him.

"Where do you live?" he asked.

I hesitated, and he groaned in disgust. "Give me a break, Natalie. I'm not going to stalk you. Trust me, I have better things to do than spend my time hanging around your house hoping to catch your attention. I don't care how cool you are."

Yeesh. Could he be more any more hostile? At the snide look on his face, I changed my mind. His glasses were geeky and I didn't like guys with blond hair. And he was arrogant. So there. "I don't think I'm cool."

He ignored my protest. "I don't want to wait around after school until you get done with practice. I have things to do."

What sort of things did a guy like Matt do? Did he go home and make up Excel spreadsheets? Program computers? "So what do you suggest?"

"If you'd tell me where you live, I might be able to help."

I rattled off my address. There was no need to to aggravate the situation any further. It was obvious I didn't have to worry about him stalking me. He'd made it perfectly clear what he thought of athletes, and he'd lumped me in with the rest of them. Well, why not? Obviously, I fit right in. I was just another dumb jock who didn't consort with the brains.

"That's not too far from my house. I could come over later. About seven?"

I was about to agree, when I thought of my parents. How was I going to explain his presence? If they knew he was a tutor, they'd take that memo off Ms. Olsen's desk and hand deliver it to the principal.

Wait a sec. Tonight they had plans at some function downtown. Mom had told me to catch a ride home from practice because she couldn't pick me up. "Seven works." For tonight. We were going to have to find somewhere else to study in the future.

Like maybe in a cave or something. Nowhere that anyone could find us.

He shoved his books in his backpack. "I'll see you at seven then." And without another word, he slung his bag over his shoulder and left me standing at the table.

Somehow I felt like I'd been ditched. Weird. And ridiculous. Ugh! Just because Matt was smarter than me didn't mean he was better.

Even if he thought so. Tonight was so not going to be fun.

But right now, I had to get back to practice and my new friends.

I sprinted all the way through the school, across two parking lots and past the football field to the track, but no one was there.

Gone already? There was no sign that cross-country practice had even occurred, except for my water bottle sitting on the bleachers where I'd left it after Valerie had invited me to stretch with them.

So was that it? What if Coach Thompson had told the team where I was? What would happen at practice tomorrow? Should I sit with Valerie and her friends again, or wait for an invite? It was a tough call. If I waited for an invite, they might take it as a slight. But, if I sat down with them without an invite, they might be offended.

If only I'd been able to run with them today, then I'd know how to act. My shoulders slumped and a lump clogged my throat. I'd been so close to having friends again, and now I had nothing except a tutor who thought I was stupid.

"Natalie?"

I spun around to find Zach standing behind me, still wearing his workout stuff. Zach!? He knew my name? Oh, *wow.* "Hi."

"What happened to you at practice today?"

He'd noticed I wasn't there? I was going to die right now. "I had a crisis."

"What kind of crisis?"

Oh, I found out I'm totally stupid and I need a tutor, why? "Um . . . it's kinda personal."

Zach lifted a brow and I felt like an idiot. This situation was already getting out of control! How was I going to avoid telling people about tutoring for the whole rest of the season?

I had no idea, but I'd better figure out something fast.

"Need a ride home?"

I looked over my shoulder to see who Zach was talking to. No one except us. "Me?"

He nodded.

The urge to jump up and down and scream my head off seized me, but then I heard Allie's voice in my head. *Be cool.*

Right. I could do that. I flipped my bangs out of my face. "Sure, I could use a ride, I guess." Did that sound casual enough? Too casual? Would he think I didn't like him? Should I have sounded more enthusiastic? Or did he already realize I was madly in love with him from the tone of my voice? Or . . .

"You going to shower?"

He thought I needed a shower? Since when would Zach care if I was sweaty? He was sweatier than I was. "Why? Do I need one?"

He laughed. "I have no idea. I was figuring out timing. I'm going to take a shower, so I'll meet you in the parking lot in ten minutes. Is that enough time?"

Crud. I was such an idiot. "Yeah, that's fine." As if Zach had been thinking about snuggling with me and been giving me a hint to get rid of the sweat. "I'll meet you in the parking lot." I took off running toward the locker rooms before he could see me blush with embarrassment.

I didn't need to shower since I hadn't worked out. I changed quickly, put on makeup and brushed my hair, and made it to the parking lot in seven minutes. Perfect. I didn't want to keep him waiting.

Zach sauntered out of the locker room almost fifteen minutes later. For those who are math challenged, like me, that's twenty-two minutes. Not ten.

He lifted a brow. "You're out here already? Most girls take forever in the locker room."

Oh, wow. Was that a total slam that I wasn't girly enough? *Please don't let Zach be one of those guys who thinks of me only as a pal.* I wanted him to notice I was a girl! Obviously, changing in seven minutes wasn't the way to do it. Next time I was going to take a book into the locker room and keep him waiting for a much longer time.

And I was going to have to talk to my friends. I

needed to find out more appropriate girl behavior. They'd all landed boyfriends, so they must be doing something right.

Zach nodded at a Jeep with no top. "That's mine."

"This is so awesome." I threw my bag in the back and swung up. "I totally want this kind of car."

He shot me another look. "Most girls worry that it'll mess up their hair."

Gah. Another mistake? I'd only been with him two minutes! "Yeah, well, um . . ." Was he thinking that I didn't like him because I didn't care about my hair when I was with him and because I didn't spend time primping?

He shrugged. "It's cool."

Cool? As in, I won't kick you out of my car? Or cool, as in, I like that you're different from other girls? Or cool, as in, wait until I tell my friends about what an idiot you are?

After I gave him directions to my house (two guys in one afternoon!) I decided not to say anything else for the entire ride home so I couldn't screw up again before I had a chance to talk to my friends. This year was going to be different for me, no matter what. I was on a new team with guys who didn't all consider me a buddy, and I was going to develop a new reputation if it killed me.

"You run JV last year?"

How was I supposed to be silent if he asked me questions? "Yes." Safe answer. Hadn't screwed up yet.

"Was Sunday your PR?"

He wanted to know my personal record? Why? "I had a race that was faster last year."

"So you're legit?"

"Legit?"

"You're really that good?"

I shrugged and tried not to grin. *Zach thinks I'm good. Zach thinks I'm good. Zach thinks I'm good.*

"You win many races last season?"

"Yeah."

He cocked a brow at me. "It'll be different on varsity. You won't always be running in the front."

"I figured that out." Sure, I'd scored second for the team, but I'd actually come in tenth. Fortunately, our top five runners all came in pretty high, so we won the meet. I'd been running in a pack the whole time and had been bumped more than once.

"You need to practice running when you're not the fastest."

"That's why I race." I realized I was jiggling my legs, as if Zach was making me nervous or something. *Be cool, Natalie.*

"Running with me will make you train harder. If you want to double, I run in the mornings before school. If you're around at six-thirty or seven, we can hook up."

Hook up? I'd love to hook up with Zach. And I'm not talking about running. "Maybe I'll swing by." Yeah, in between tutoring sessions. Gak!

Much too soon Zach pulled into my driveway. My mom and dad's cars were still in the driveway, but they would be heading out soon. I hoped. If not, I was going to sit out in the street and tackle Matt when he arrived to keep him from coming into the house. "Thanks for the ride."

"Anytime. I live in this end of town, so it was convenient. Let me know if you need a ride again."

Hoo, yeah. How about every day?

No, I was supposed to be cool. Besides, I'd already changed too quickly and I didn't worry enough about my hair, so he totally wasn't hitting on me.

Yet.

I was definitely going to have to change that.

3

My parents left four minutes before Matt arrived. Four minutes! I was panicking! My mom hadn't been able to find her favorite pearl earrings, and I'd gone on a mad search to locate them. My dad was making phone calls and my mom was moaning and groaning.

Thank heavens I was there to straighten them out. I found the earrings, rounded them up and herded them out the door.

I was still standing on the front step when Matt rode up the driveway on his bike. He was wearing a bike helmet, had a strap around his left pant leg to keep his jeans from snagging on the chain, and he had his backpack over both shoulders.

So uncool.

He coasted to a stop in front of me. "Waiting for me?"

Ack! *So uncool* to be caught waiting for him, especially since I wasn't! "No. My parents just left so I was out here watching them drive away . . ." Crud. How stupid did that sound?

He flipped his leg over his bike. "You always watch your parents leave?"

Hey! I was the one who was supposed to be cool here, not him! So how was he turning this around so successfully? "No. I never watch them drive off." Yeah, that was a witty comeback. Point for Natalie. Hah.

"Can I bring my bike inside? I don't want to leave it outside."

"This isn't a bad neighborhood."

"It's my only bike."

Get a little more protective of a pile of metal and rubber. "Fine."

I held the door open for him while he wheeled the bike inside, catching a whiff of something that smelled good. Aftershave? He was only fifteen. Surely he didn't shave. Cologne? It was so faint, it was difficult to tell. All I knew was that I liked it. Weird to be liking the smell of Matt. He was my tutor, not some hottie.

"Where to? Kitchen?"

"Sure." I led the way to the kitchen. I couldn't believe I was about to be tutored. Here I was on the verge of a social crisis, in desperate need of advice from my friends on how to be girly, and I was stuck with Matt, learning geometry. And I was going to do this every day for the entire semester?

No way. I'd never survive.

The only option was to prove to Matt and Ms. Olsen that I didn't need a tutor. No problem. I didn't need one anyway, right?

While Matt pulled books out of his backpack, I retrieved mine from the family room, where I'd dumped my bag unopened when I got home. I carried my math book and a notebook back into the kitchen. "How long is this going to take?"

He started flipping open cabinets until he found the glasses, then grabbed one. "As long as it takes. I already did the rest of my homework, so I have all night."

I nearly dropped my book. It was only seven and he'd already done all his homework? Was he kidding? I hadn't even unzipped my bag, let alone figured out what I had to do. "Yeah, me too."

"Good." He opened the fridge and pulled out a can of root beer. Tossed some ice in the glass, grabbed the cookie tin from the counter and then brought it all over to the table.

"Help yourself," I said. Nice manners, dude.

"I don't expect you to wait on me."

Oh. When he put it that way, it was sort of okay. I guess. Wasn't it? He was totally confusing me.

He nodded. "Sit."

I sat. Not because I would do what he said, but because I felt like sitting and his suggestion had coincided with my desire to sit. So there.

He pulled out his assignment notebook, then started flipping through his book. I sat there until he shot a meaningful look at my book. Then I immediately opened mine. Duh. What was my problem? My brain had stopped functioning merely because I was in the presence of a smart boy? *Get it together, Natalie.*

I opened to the assignment and read the first problem. It made no sense whatsoever.

Matt scooted his chair around the table so he was sitting next to me. "Why don't you start working on it, and I'll watch you. It'll help me figure out where you are."

Start? But the problem made no sense. "Um . . ."

He picked up a pencil and held it out. "You'll need this."

"Thanks." I felt sweat beading on my forehead. The pressure! It was one thing not to have any idea how to answer the problems when I was alone and no one had to know how stupid I was. But to look totally stupid in front of someone else? Especially a guy who was in my class? Forget it!

I threw down the pencil. "I'm hungry. I think I'll make a sandwich. Want one?"

He grabbed my wrist as I started to push my chair back. "I'm here to work, not sit around while you procrastinate. It's fine if you do that on your own time, but I have too much to do to waste time while you fart around."

Okay, my humiliation had reached new levels. "You're a study geek."

"Yep. And you appear to be a stereotypical dumb jock. I'm being paid to help you. So sit down." His eyes were flashing, and I knew he hadn't appreciated the geek comment.

"I'm not a dumb jock." I sat back down and folded my arms across my chest.

He handed me the pencil. "Prove it." He grinned. "A little geometry humor."

I rolled my eyes. "So not funny."

His smile faded. "No matter how hard you try, you're not getting rid of me. I want Ms. Olsen to hire me next summer to work on a research project, and this is my chance to impress her. So you're stuck with me and I *will* make you pass this class."

Great. So he had incentive to stalk me with a math book for the rest of the semester. Unless I could get straight As right away; then there'd be no need for him. I grabbed the pencil. "Fine. Watch this." I read the problem again.

And then again.

Then I drew my proof table.

Then I read it again. Um . . .

"You don't know where to begin?"

"Of course I do," I snapped. "I'm thinking."

"Ah." He totally didn't believe me. Too smart, I guess.

I decided I hated smart guys. "Okay, fine. I don't know where to start."

"Really?" He looked so surprised I wanted to punch him.

"Are you being paid to make me feel stupid, too?"

He had the grace to look embarrassed. "No, sorry. It's no problem. This stuff is hard." He leaned closer so his shoulder was touching mine. "Okay, so let's start at the beginning."

Good. The beginning. Sounded like a good place to start.

He pointed to the page. "See this? What do you make of this?"

I frowned. "It's a triangle. And some extra lines pointing out."

He lifted a brow. "What kind of triangle?"

"With three sides." I was starting to sweat now. He was totally going to know I had no idea what I was doing. That I was stupid.

He pulled back and looked at me. "Are you being intentionally difficult or do you really not know?"

I suddenly felt like crying. "Why do you keep doing that? So I'm dumb. So I don't understand. There, are you happy now? I admitted it. Shut up and leave me alone."

Matt leaned back in his chair and ran his hand through his hair. "Listen, I'm sorry. I didn't mean to make you feel stupid. I have to find out exactly how much you understand so I know where to start." He cleared his throat. "With your . . . um . . . attitude earlier, I thought maybe you were being intentionally difficult."

I wiped a traitorous tear off my cheek. "Well, I'm not. I'm stupid. Okay? Happy? You're smarter than me. I don't understand this at all and I hate it and I hate having to think about it because I can't do it!"

Matt shifted in his chair and looked like he'd rather be getting a cavity filled than sitting here with me. Good. I hoped he was suffering. I'd make him earn his seven bucks an hour. "Um . . . so how about if I start by explaining some basic concepts?"

"Basic? I might not be able to understand them." I blinked hard and ordered my tears away.

"Sure you can." He pulled the book closer to him and flipped to the start of the chapter. "I'm a great tutor."

"With a big ego."

He shrugged. "You should be glad you got me. I'm good." He scanned the page for a couple seconds, no doubt doing some speed reading of this very *basic* stuff. "Okay, you ready?"

I nodded, and felt a little glimmer of hope. If he was a great tutor, then maybe he could help me. "Um . . . Matt?"

"Yeah?" He jotted some notes down on his paper.

"You're not going to tell anyone, are you?"

He looked up, and I noticed he had really blue eyes. "Tell anyone what?"

"That you're tutoring me?"

He cocked his head. "You want to keep it a secret?"

"No, I don't care." I hesitated. "I mean, yeah. If my parents knew I was being tutored, they'd pull me off the team."

"We wouldn't want that, would we?"

I gave him my best annoyed look. "No, 'we' wouldn't." I decided not to go into how my social life depended on not being known as so stupid that I needed a tutor.

He shrugged. "It's not interesting enough for me to discuss with other people."

Ouch. Total slam. "Good." But at least I'd gotten the desired result. A promise of silence.

"Is that it?"

How could he sound so disdainful of everything not related to a burning need to learn? "Yeah."

He continued to look at me. "You're putting up with the tutoring thing so you can stay on the team? Not because you care about your grades or anything?"

"Exactly. Running is so important to me . . ." My voice faded at the look on his face. "What?"

"Good to know your motivation." He didn't sound like he was impressed with it.

"Hey, Matt. Not everyone is obsessed with school and grades like you are."

"Your loss." He nodded at the book. "You ready to focus? We have a lot to go over."

I felt my chest tighten again at the thought of tackling geometry. I hated it. Hated it, hated it, hated it. Because I couldn't do it. Not at all.

He lifted his brow. "You look sick."

"Thanks." I took a deep breath. "I'm fine. Let's start." *Think of running. Think of Zach. Think of Valerie and her cool friends. It's all worth it.*

"You sure? I don't want you to puke on me."

I laughed at the comical look of horror on his face. "I'm not going to puke. I save that for after hard races."

His look of horror intensified. "Seriously?"

"Yeah."

"And you like this sport?"

"Well, I don't particularly enjoy the puking part, but yeah, I like the sport."

He shook his head. "Remind me not to go watch a race. Seeing a bunch of kids spilling their guts isn't high on my list of fun activities."

Such a geek. "I suppose you avoid sweat too."

"I ride a bike everywhere."

Yeah, good point. Still a geek. "So are you going to help me or what?"

"Yeah." He pulled the book over and pointed to a list of words. "We're going to go over each of these terms until you understand them, okay? And you have to stop me if you start to feel lost. It serves no purpose if you pretend you understand and you don't. Got it?"

I lifted a brow at the perfunctory recital. "You've given that speech before, huh?"

"Every time. Doesn't usually work, but I'm serious. If you don't know what the heck I'm talking about, tell me. Okay?"

"You already know how dumb I am, so I guess there's no point in hiding it, huh?" I laughed weakly to hide my discomfort.

"Exactly."

Jerk. That was his perfect opportunity to tell me that no, I wasn't actually stupid. I was merely geometry-challenged.

He pointed to the first word on the list. "Obtuse angle. Tell me what you can about obtuse angles."

Nothing. I knew nothing about obtuse angles. I did

know that Matt seemed intent on proving just how stupid I was.

So good to know we agreed on something.

I was concentrating so hard that I didn't even hear my parents walk into the house.

"Natalie! Who's this?"

My head snapped up and I stared at them. "You're home already?"

"It's ten-thirty."

Matt cursed under his breath. "Ten-thirty? I gotta get home."

My dad blocked the door. "What's going on here? Who is this?"

Oh, *no*. How was I going to explain Matt? Our books were open, and there were notes sprawled all across the table. It was totally obvious we'd been studying. "Um . . . this is Matt Turner."

Matt shook my parents' hands, then continued to shove stuff into his backpack.

"You two were studying?" My mom sounded too casual. She was totally digging for info.

Matt looked up. "Yes, I'm her . . ."

"Boyfriend!" I shouted and jumped to my feet. "Matt's my new boyfriend."

His mouth dropped open and he gaped at me.

Oh, crud. He was totally going to blow it. I grabbed his arm and shot him my most pleading look. I'll do anything for you, I mentally promised him, hoping he was psychic. *Please go along with this*. I zipped his backpack up and pushed it at him. "You have to be going. I'll see you at school tomorrow."

"Natalie . . ." His voice dripped with warning.

"Tomorrow. I'll see you tomorrow. Thanks for studying with me." I practically carried him and his bike out of the house, slamming the door shut behind him.

I leaned back against the door for a moment, trying to collect myself. I was in such trouble with Matt tomorrow.

Then my parents walked into the front hall and I knew I was in trouble with them too. They totally knew I was lying. I'm sure they could smell tutor dripping from every pore of my desperate body. "Um . . ."

"Why didn't you tell us you had a boyfriend?"

I blinked. They'd bought it. "Um . . . because we just started dating."

My parents exchanged glances and I crossed my fingers behind my back.

It was my mom who spoke for them. "We're not comfortable with the two of you being in the house unchaperoned."

I nearly laughed. As if Matt was going to try to kiss me! "I understand."

"And we're very bothered by the fact that you didn't tell us he was coming over."

Uh-oh. I sensed an ultimatum coming on. What if they banned me from dating him? Then how was I going to explain it if I continued to hang out with him? *Think, Natalie, think.* "He's a straight-A student."

My mom lifted her eyebrows. "Really?"

"Yeah, he's a major math geek."

My dad was a physics professor at a local university and my mom was an ex-accountant who now owned a successful chain of beauty salons. They would totally love it if I dated a guy who was a math and science nerd and got good grades. The perfect child they'd never had.

"He's a science geek too. Did I mention straight As?"

My parents looked really interested now. They'd always been concerned that I'd shown far more aptitude and interest in sports than school, so they had to be thinking that maybe Matt would be a good influence on me. "And he isn't into sports at all. Thinks they're dumb, actually."

They looked at each other and did some sort of silent communication. Then my mom looked at me. "Why don't you invite him to dinner so we can get to know him?"

Dinner? That meant Matt would have to keep up the charade. He'd never do it. Ever! "Um . . ."

"It's either dinner or you don't get to see him again. You aren't having a boyfriend who we don't know and approve of."

Oh, this was great. I was really in deep now. "I'll see what he says."

"Good."

Yeah, great. How in the heck was I going to get myself out of *this* mess?

4

My wonderful friends were able to meet for a quick emergency session of "Save Natalie" at two o'clock, between school and practice. Fortunately, Allie and Frances both got out at one o'clock—didn't private-school kids ever go to class?

Blue and I had met them after last period, and we congregated in the corner of the cafeteria. It was too rainy to meet outside—yuck!

"So, what's up?" Allie had become a fixture at my practice lately. Since she'd started dating Tad, who ran cross country for another school, she came to my practice so she could learn about the sport and talk with him about it. Gah. How pathetic was that? Taking on his interests just because she was dating him?

It was amazing I'd managed to get them all together without any boyfriends in tow. Of course, Blue's boyfriend was in college, but he was going to Harvard, so he was around a lot. Guess that's what happens when you attend college only twenty minutes from your true love, huh? Gag.

It didn't help that Frances's boyfriend went to Boston University, so she and Blue were always hopping the T to ride down there and visit them.

I'd never gone because I had practice, and Allie hadn't gone because she was hanging with her boyfriend. Not that we'd been invited. I don't think either of them wanted to share their time with their precious boyfriends.

Anyway, none of their boyfriends were around, which was why they were all boy-less at two o'clock on a Tuesday afternoon.

"Okay, here's the scoop." I had decided not to tell them about the tutoring/fake-boyfriend thing. I mean, sure, they were my friends, but the tutoring thing was too embarrassing. "I need to impress a guy. I need to get him to notice me."

Allie sat up. "It's that guy from practice, isn't it? Zach whassiname?"

My cheeks got hot, and she whooped. "I knew it!" She turned to Blue and Frances. "He's totally cute. Natalie knows how to pick 'em."

"Shh!" I smacked her arm while I looked around the cafeteria to make sure no one was within listening distance. Mucho embarrassing to be caught talking about Zach's hotness. "How do you get a guy to notice you as a girl, instead of a buddy?"

"Kiss him," Allie announced.

Blue nodded. "That would definitely send a message."

Frances rolled her eyes. "Don't even think about kissing him! He'll think you're a slut and he won't respect you."

Allie spun around to face Frances. "That's ridiculous. One kiss doesn't make a girl a slut."

"Hey!" I didn't want this to turn into an argument between Frances and Allie about how much to put out. Their takes on the situation were kind of ironic, given that Frances was dating the college guy and Allie was dating the high-school sophomore, huh? "I can't kiss him. I need to get his interest first. I already learned I have to go slow in the locker room. What else?"

My friends stared at me.

"What?" I shifted under their gaze.

"What in the world are you talking about?" Allie asked. "Go slow in the locker room?"

"I have to spend time primping and let him know I'm doing it."

"Oh." They all relaxed. "That makes sense," Allie said. "I had no idea what you were referring to."

"And I learned I should worry about my hair."

Allie eyed the feature in question. "Not just worry about it. Do something about it, too."

I touched my hair. "I blew it dry this morning. It doesn't look okay?"

"It looks like the same wild mop it always does," Allie said.

"Ignore her. Your hair is fine and you don't need makeup," Frances said. "What you need to do is be mean to him. Keep him in his place, and then he'll appreciate you."

"No," Allie said. "Make out with him as soon as you can and definitely get a haircut. I'll take you to my stylist if you want. She's fab."

Blue held up her hand. "Ignore them both. Be yourself. If he doesn't like you the way you are, then it's not right. Kiss him if you feel like it. If you don't, don't. It shouldn't matter." She sat up. "In fact, you should become friends with him first. That's the best way."

Were they kidding? They were all contradicting each other!

I leaned back in my chair as they launched into a debate about the best way to get a guy to notice you. "Um, hello?"

They ignored me.

"Hey!" I smacked my fist on the table and only got a rush of pain for the effort. They didn't even notice. "I already slept with him."

Three heads spun toward me so fast I wouldn't have been surprised to see them all go flying across the room. Total shocked silence from my three virgin friends who all had serious boyfriends.

I grinned. "I was kidding. It was the only way to get your attention." I plunged ahead before they could regain their composure and interrupt me. "Blue, I always become friends with guys and it never goes any further than that. That's why I need the help. Frances, I'm not going to be mean. It's not my style." I looked at Allie.

"Zach made a couple comments about how I'm not like other girls, mostly because I wasn't primping and worrying about my hair. So I was thinking that was why nothing has gone beyond friends with all these other guys? Because I'm too much like a guy?"

Frances snorted. "You have boobs, Natalie. You're not a guy."

"Then why don't any guys notice me?"

"Because they're not right for you," Blue said.

"Or because they're stupid. Guys can be stupid," Allie added.

Stupid. I wasn't too high on that word right now. "Stupid isn't a bad thing."

Frances rolled her eyes. "Oh, come on, Natalie. Stupid isn't good either."

I swallowed and picked my fingernails. "I just wanted to know how to be feminine." *Natalie is stupid. Natalie is stupid. Natalie is stupid*. I clapped my hands over my hears to try to drum out the noise.

"Not by doing that."

Yeah, I looked cool cringing like I was hearing voices. I immediately dropped my hands. "I need to know how to act like a girl. Will you guys help?"

Allie was the first to volunteer, and Frances and Blue chimed right in with their willingness to contribute to the cause.

Awesome. I loved my friends. "How about Saturday? We can have a girl's day?"

Blue shook her head. "I'm going to spend the day with Colin."

Frances nodded. "And I'm going to watch Theo play football."

"And Tad's family is taking me shopping so I can buy my own camping equipment."

Okay, then. "I can't go Sunday because I have a meet."

"Hmm . . ." Allie pulled out her PDA and scrolled through. "I'm free the next Saturday. Anyone else?"

"Football," Frances said.

"Oh, come on, Frances," Blue said. "I think he can practice without you glomming on to him on the sidelines."

Frances glared at Blue. "I don't get to see him all week. You just don't appreciate his talent because he's your brother."

"What happened to The Ledge?" Blue asked. "Shouldn't you at least be trying to give the pretense of having your own identity?"

"I have my own identity. I'm on the newspaper, I have great grades. Theo's grades went up an entire point when he started dating me."

Great. Just great. My friends arguing about their boyfriends. Left me out in the cold, didn't it? I sighed. "Let's plan on next Saturday. Whoever can be there, great. As long as Allie comes, that's what matters."

Blue and Frances snapped offended glares my way. "You only care about Allie?"

"I didn't mean it that way. Allie's the one who offered to set me up with her stylist, and we all know she's the expert when it comes to makeup and fashion, right?"

They shared disgruntled looks, but shrugged. No one could disagree that Allie was the fashion queen.

"But I want all of you there," I added. "I just can't wait a month until all of you have time for me." I saw Valerie and her friends walk through the cafeteria on their way to practice. "I gotta go. Practice." Without waiting for a response, I grabbed my bag and jumped to my feet. I hoped Valerie or Marcie would notice me, because I wasn't sure if I should go up to them.

They didn't, and I ended up walking about twenty feet behind them all the way to the gym feeling like a total idiot.

They even let the door to the locker room slam in my face, but it was because they hadn't noticed I was there.

At least that's what I kept telling myself. Before today, it would have been intentional, but I was hoping it was different now.

I picked a locker on the same row as them, but way at the end. Usually, I changed in a whole other part of the locker room, but I didn't want to offend them if they were thinking I should be with them. But I didn't want to get in trouble by being too close to them either. So I picked a happy medium, and I was rewarded with a brilliant smile from Valerie when she noticed me.

"Natalie! What happened to you yesterday?"

"Um . . ." Why hadn't I spent last night coming up with a good excuse? Instead, I'd spent the night lying in bed wondering how I was going to solve my little predicament with Matt. He'd barely said two words to me in geometry class, not even to set a time or place to meet tonight.

Did that mean he was going to show up at my house at seven? What if he was planning to come clean to my parents? Crud. I had to find a way to head him off.

Or maybe he was abandoning the tutoring job. Yeah, that was it! Excellent! Then I wouldn't have to finagle the dinner invite with my parents.

I realized Valerie was waiting, as were her friends. "Family crisis. My mom had a car accident."

"Oh. Is she okay? Can you still drive the car?"

"Yeah, they're both fine." Not that it mattered, since I didn't have my driver's license, but there was no need to remind Valerie-the-senior of that.

"Good." She nodded and went back to changing.

Either I had to prepare my mom for a lot of car accidents, or I was going to have to come up with a better excuse.

Valerie and her friends waited for me, and we all walked out together. Marcie even held the door for me. Score!

We walked across the field as a bunch, and I was in the middle. Sure, I was too scared to talk, but to an outsider, I was in.

An outsider like Zach, who was watching us approach. Yes! I touched my pigtails to make sure they were cute, then I grinned at him.

He smiled back, and then I caught my toe in the turf, tripped and crashed into Valerie's back. "Sorry."

She gave me a weird look. "No problem. As long as you don't trip when you're racing, it's fine with me."

Yet another reminder that my social future depended on my legs. Good thing I was up to the challenge.

"Natalie!"

We all looked to the right at the sound of my name being bellowed. Matt stood on the edge of the field. He was on his bike, wearing his helmet and glasses, with his jeans bunched up by that little tie thing again.

"You know him?" Valerie asked.

"He's stalking me," I said. "Let me go get rid of him." I broke into a jog and raced toward Matt. He was *so* banned from coming to practice! "What are you doing here?"

"As your boyfriend, I can come see you practice, can't I?" There was no humor in his gaze.

"I'm really sorry about that. I panicked."

"And used me."

"No! I just . . . well . . . I wasn't thinking." I eyed him hopefully. "But it's not so bad, is it? I mean, maybe you could keep up that charade with my parents? Would that be cool?"

His gaze darkened. "No, it wouldn't."

Darn it. This was really not going well. "Please? What does it hurt you?"

He lifted a brow. "You think you're so cool that it could only enhance my reputation to be associated with you, even as a lie?"

"No! I don't think I'm cool!" How did this conversation get so screwed up? "Listen, can we talk about this later? I need to go practice."

His gaze flicked over my shoulder. "Fine. Town library at seven?"

"Not my house?"

"Not until you straighten things out with your parents. I'm not interested in being used."

"I'm not using you!"

"Then what would you call it?"

"Um . . ." Good question. I glanced over my shoulder to see if practice had started and saw Zach on his way over. "Oh my God."

Matt followed my gaze. "Who's that?"

"I totally like him. You have to be cool."

He arched a brow behind his glasses. "I'm surprised you think I have it in me to be cool."

"Shut up, Matt. I can't mess this up. Don't you dare tell him about the tutoring thing. Just be quiet." I broke into a smile. "Hi, Zach."

Zach nodded at me, then eyed Matt. "Who are you?"

Matt hesitated for a sec, then he threw his arm around my shoulder and hauled me up against him. "Natalie's boyfriend."

What? I whirled around to kick him in the shin, but the second I was facing him, he grabbed me by the shoulders and kissed me. Then he released me and flipped me a grin. "See you tonight, darlin'."

He took off on his bike before I could injure him, leaving me standing with a very surprised Zach. "I didn't realize you had a boyfriend."

"Um . . . yeah . . . well . . ." Seeing as how I might be seen with Matt on repeated occasions for the rest of the season, I had to be very careful about how I dealt with this. One bad choice could expose me. "He's not really my boyfriend . . . he's actually . . . um . . ."

"Zach! Natalie! Get over here!" Coach Thompson hollered at us, giving me a reprieve before I had to come up with a coherent explanation for that nightmare.

When Zach and I rejoined the team, I quickly dropped to the ground and leaned over my hamstring. Matt Turner was dead meat when I saw him tonight.

Dead.

Meat.

I slammed my backpack on the table, making Matt jump backwards. "Good. I hope I scared the crap out of you."

He grinned and laced his fingers behind his head. "Doesn't feel so good to be on the other side, does it?"

"What was that about? Didn't you hear me say that I *liked* Zach? And now he thinks I have a boyfriend? How exactly do you think that's going to help me snag him?"

"Did it ever occur to you that I might already have a girlfriend?"

No response came to mind at all.

"You thought I was too much of a brain to have my own life?" he asked.

"No . . . I didn't think at all. One way or the other." I swallowed. "Do you have a girlfriend?"

"Yes."

Ouch. So even brainiacs had significant others? Was I the only one on the entire planet who was single? "Really? You're not just saying that?" I dropped into the seat across from him. "You're making it up."

He took his wallet out of his back pocket and tossed it across the table.

"You want me to look in your wallet?" At his nod, I opened it. Fifteen bucks in cash, an ATM card, a student ID and a photo. I pulled it out and looked at it. The girl looked our age, with straight blond hair, a nice smile and a perfect nose. She was totally cute, and not at all geeky looking. "This is your girlfriend?" Wow.

"Read the back."

I flipped it over. "Matt. I'll always love you. Liz."

I hadn't seen this twist coming. How was I going to cope with this one?

5

What to do? I carefully replaced the picture, stalling for time, but when I handed it back to him, I had no idea what to do. "So, I guess the boyfriend thing is off, then, huh?"

"It would be off anyway." He shoved the wallet back in his pocket. "I'm your tutor, and that's it. If you have a problem with telling people you're being tutored, that's your problem, not mine. I personally like being known as your tutor. Enhances my reputation."

"As a brain."

"Exactly. I consider that a good thing."

Was he arrogant or what? I was used to athletes who thought the world revolved around them because of their muscles, but never a smart person who thought his IQ made him better than everyone else. Totally annoying. "Does Liz go to our school?"

"No."

"What school? Doesn't she get mad that you have all this tutoring stuff going on? When do you see her?"

He opened his math book. "She's in London for a year with her parents. Her dad was sent there for his job." My cell phone rang then. Blue. Excellent. I'd take any excuse I could to regroup. "Give me a sec?" I turned away before he could answer. "Hello?"

"You have a boyfriend? What's that all about? Named Matt Turner? Not Zach? What was today all about, trying to snag Zach? We want details, girl, and we want them now!"

"Um . . . Blue? This isn't a good time."

"Frances and Allie are here, and we expect you to get your butt over to my house within ten minutes to fill us in. I can't believe I had to hear about it from my mom who heard it from your mom. Ten minutes." She hung up before I could reply. Crud. This was getting way out of control.

Matt was grinning. "I heard that."

"Why are you laughing? If everyone starts thinking I'm dating you, then they're going to think *you're* dating *me.* Won't Liz get mad?"

"Oh, I can explain it. She's cool. She'd think it's a riot." He chuckled. "Guess you're getting payback for that lie, huh? How does it feel?"

"Shut up." I folded my arms across my chest and tried to make my brain function. My friends and my parents and my cross-country team all thought I was dating Matt, and since I had to keep hanging out with him every friggin' day, how was I going to explain it away? Or maybe I didn't need to . . . "You think Zach will be more likely to notice me if he believes I have a boyfriend? It might make him more aware that I'm a girl, don't you think?"

Matt's grin faded and he looked uncomfortable—you know that look boys always get when you talk about relationships and stuff. "Beats me."

I rubbed my chin. "That might work. We could pretend to date for a while, enough for Zach to want me. Then when we finish with the tutoring, we could 'break up' and Zach could finally have me for his own."

"Are you deaf? I have a girlfriend."

"Well, if she's out of town, then the boyfriend thing shouldn't matter, right? Besides, you already said you could explain it."

"Yeah, but . . ."

"You have to hang out with me anyway, right? It wouldn't require you to do anything other than not deny it." I narrowed my gaze. "No more kissing me, though."

He grinned again. "You liked that? I thought it was a good move."

I had to admit, he'd done a great job of making the whole thing appear like the real deal. Not that I'd tell him that. "You're not a good kisser."

"Trust me, that wasn't all I've got."

I suddenly felt very embarrassed. Matt the geeky brain with some serious kissing skills and a hot girlfriend? Not at all what I'd have expected.

It didn't matter though. Totally irrelevant to what I needed to convince him to do. I leaned back in my chair and gave him my "I'm tough" look that I send other competitors before a race. "What do you want?"

"To get to work. I don't want to spend all night here." He unzipped my backpack and pulled my book out.

"I'll bribe you to pretend you're my boyfriend."

"Let's start with chapter three." He opened my book and thumbed through to the right page. "We'll start with a recap of what we learned in class today, okay?"

"My dad's a physics professor at a local college."

I saw a flicker of interest on his face before he spun my book around to face me. "Got a pencil and paper? Ready to take notes?"

"He always hires a couple of people to do research for him over the summer." I crossed my fingers behind my back, and my ankles under the table. Based on Matt's math interest, I was hoping he was also a science aficionado. Didn't math and science go together?

"I'm sure he hires college kids." Matt pulled out the syllabus. "I figure we'll spend the first half of tonight on tomorrow's assignment, then we'll spend the rest of the time going over stuff from the beginning of the semester. We'll keep splitting our sessions like that until you understand everything we've done so far this year."

"He wants you to come to dinner. So he can get to know you."

That got his attention. "Really?"

"Yeah. My parents are hoping you'll be a good influence on me. They'll do anything to keep you around if they believe you can get me to take school more seriously."

Matt tapped the end of his pen on the table. "How do I know you're telling the truth?"

"Come to dinner and find out for yourself. I'll talk you up from the job perspective, and then you can grill him and see if it's legit. If it is, then you have incentive to stick around and be my boyfriend."

"And then when we 'break up'?"

"I'll make sure it's amicable so he doesn't hate you."

He stuck the end of the pen between his teeth and chewed. I could see the glow of interest in his eyes, even behind his glasses. "If, and I'm only saying if, I go to dinner and I get convinced that the job opportunity is legit, then you can't 'break up' with me until I get the offer. And then after that, the 'break up' will be on my terms so it doesn't mess up the job."

"Hey! I have some standards too. The 'breakup' has to make me look desirable to Zach as well."

He nodded slowly. "We can probably float that."

"Not 'probably.' It's a deal breaker. I want Zach."

"And I want a job."

"I know."

We stared at each other for about an eternity. Then I passed out from holding my breath and gave myself a concussion when I hit the corner of the table.

Just kidding.

I was holding my breath, though.

Finally, he shrugged. "It's worth checking out. When's dinner?"

Somehow, I managed to restrain myself from jump-ing on top of the table and screaming victory. Instead, I called my mom. "Mom, I'm with Matt right now, and he said he'd be up for dinner. When?"

I heard her talk to my dad, then she came back on. "Friday night? Seven o'clock? Then maybe he can stay for the evening and we can all play games."

Gah. How embarrassing. Games with my family? I hit mute on the phone. "Seven on Friday? Then some family game time?" I added the last as a joke, but Matt nodded.

"Sounds good. It'll give me some quality interaction time with your dad."

Super. So we were on for family game night. All my friends were out on dates, and I was going to be playing Trivial Pursuit with my parents and my fake boyfriend? Things were looking worse by the minute, and it was all Ms. Olsen's fault. I unmuted the phone. "We'll be there."

"Don't sound so excited about it," my mom said.

Darn. "I am excited. I'm just tired." I eyed Matt. "Matt and I are studying at the library and I'm kinda fried."

"You're studying? Again? Two nights in a row?"

I rolled my eyes. "Yeah. It's the only way I get to spend time with him, since he studies all the time. Did I tell you he gets straight As in both math and science?" I cocked an eyebrow at Matt, and he nodded his affirmation. Brain. "And he's really interested in talking to Dad about physics."

Matt grinned and I heard my mom pass the message

on to my dad. She came back on. "Dad's excited. He doesn't get many captive audiences around the dinner table."

"Matt can't wait. See ya." I hung up. "Happy? They love you already."

"It's a good start . . . if there really is a job. If there isn't, I'll tell them in the middle of dinner that I'm tutoring you."

"What? Why would you do that?"

"Because I don't like being made a fool of by jocks. So be warned and cancel dinner if it's a joke."

Yeesh. "Get a little more uptight."

"I'm not uptight. Just not interested in being battered."

"You think I'm the type to jerk you around?" Was I offended by his low opinion of me? Yes, I was quite sure I was.

"You're a jock, aren't you?"

"Get over your jock issues already."

He narrowed his eyes. "It's going to be a real treat being your boyfriend."

"Back at you with that one." I held up my book. "Shall we? I'd like to be freed from this torture as soon as possible."

"Fine with me."

As he started to talk gibberish, I remembered Blue's phone call. I was going to be in such trouble. First, I didn't tell them about Matt-the-boyfriend, and then I'd stood them up at her house?

I was going to have a lot of begging to do. The question was: Should I tell them the truth about Matt being my tutor?

That would be best.

Except there was something to be said for no longer being thought of as the loser fourth wheel who couldn't get a boyfriend of her own.

So maybe I'd let them keep on thinking it.

I looked at Matt. Or maybe I'd wait and see how Friday went.

I could only avoid my friends until I stepped onto school property the next morning. Blue was sitting on the front step, waiting for me. No, cancel that. She was stalking me, hovering in ready-to-swoop-down-and-kill-me-for-holding-out-on-them mode.

She found me crawling on my knees behind the bike rack. "Natalie! You're avoiding me?"

"Oh, there you are." I stood up and brushed off my knees. "I was looking everywhere for you."

"What happened to you last night?"

"I was with Matt when you called. And you hung up on me before I could explain."

Blue's eyes widened. "Matt the boyfriend?"

He's my tutor.

He's my boyfriend.

He's my tutor.

He's my boyfriend.

He's my tutor.

He's my boyfriend.

"Natalie?"

"Yes. Matt the boyfriend." I cringed as the words rolled off my tongue, but my guilt went away immediately at the glow of awe in Blue's eyes.

"That's so cool you have a boyfriend."

A smug smile settled on my face. "I know. And I didn't even need to have one of your boyfriends set me up. Got him on my own." I was such a liar, but it felt so good not to be the loser of the group anymore. Sure, I'd tell them the truth eventually, but I wanted to keep this feeling for just a little longer. Natalie's not a loser. Natalie's not a loser. Sounded good, didn't it?

"How could you not tell us about him?"

"Because you guys are so busy with your boyfriends that you didn't have time for me." Nothing wrong with throwing a little guilt out there.

She shot me an injured look. "That's not true."

"No? When was the last Friday night you spent with me? When was our last girls' night?"

"We were all together yesterday," Blue said. "To discuss *your* problems, I might add."

"Wow, you guys can spare twenty minutes on a Tuesday. I'm so lucky." Interesting to know that the guilt from lying put me on the defensive. Must work on that so the world doesn't hate me by the end of the semester. That's many moons of lies to turn me into a raging witch.

"Hey! You could have told us yesterday! But all you did was talk about Zach."

"I *do* like Zach."

"So, you have a boyfriend but you want advice on how to get a different guy?"

"Ah . . . well . . . it sort of looks like that, huh?" Yeesh. I never realized how complicated lying could get.

She shook her head. "Allie and Frances are going to be pissed."

"Yeah, well, sorry." Shouldn't I be the one who is pissed? They're the ones who had abandoned me for their guys.

"Saturday night then?"

I shifted my backpack to the other shoulder. "What's on Saturday night?"

"Frances, Allie and I are all going out with our boyfriends. Now that you have one, you have to bring Matt along."

My toe caught on the top step into the school and I fell on my face. "You guys have triple dates?" I wiped the dirt off my hands and tried to look cool.

"Well, yeah."

"How long has this been going on?"

She shrugged. "Since Allie started dating Tad."

Wow.

Wow.

I felt like I needed to sit down or something. I mean, I'd noticed they didn't have as much time for me now that they all had boyfriends, but I thought they were all going out separately. They'd been having all these parties and not invited me?

Natalie, the third wheel.

Natalie, so un-girly that none of their boyfriends' friends wanted to be set up with her, even for one Saturday night.

Natalie, the loser, who was also stupid.

"Nat? You in for Saturday?"

"I don't know. I'll have to check with Matt. We might have plans with his friends, though."

Blue wrinkled her nose. "His friends are more important than us?"

There was no way to stop myself from glaring at her. "Don't even start with me."

"What's wrong with you?"

"Forget it. I'll see you in class." I spun on my heel and left her standing in the hall. Good thing she didn't follow me or she might have seen my eyes getting watery. They were my best friends! How could they ditch me like this?

And to think I'd considered telling them the truth, that not only did I not have a boyfriend, but that I was also so stupid I needed a tutor.

Hah.

Fat chance of that now. No way was I admitting just how much of a loser I was.

Which meant I had a lot riding on Friday night. Not only did I need it to stay on the track team, and fool my parents, and attract Zach, but Matt as my boyfriend was also the key toward climbing back to respectability with my friends.

I walked into math class and saw Matt immediately. He was sitting in the front row, his head bent over his paper scribbling furiously. Blue was already there, sitting in the far back row with her bag on the seat next to her.

Saving it for me.

There was also an empty seat next to Matt, not that he cared whether I sat next to him. In fact, he'd probably prefer I didn't, especially since on his other side was one of his brainiac friends. It would totally cramp his style to have to admit in public that he knew stupid me without being able to explain that he's my tutor.

Blue waved and patted the desk next to her.

Matt leaned over to talk to his friend—and yes, I admit it: I had no idea what his friend's name was, even though I knew the name of every boy in the room who was an athlete or otherwise considered to be cool.

Then Ms. Olsen entered and it was decision time.

6

I walked to the front row and sat down next to Matt. "Hi."

He looked up in surprise. Then he glanced back over his shoulder to Blue (interesting that he'd noticed me and where I usually sat, yet I hadn't known his name? I hate it when guys are right) and the empty seat next to her. Then he lifted a brow behind his glasses. "Trying to prove something?"

"Like what?" I dropped my bag on the ground and unzipped it.

"I'm not sure." He didn't look happy about it. "I don't like being used."

"Yeah, you've said that before." I let my math book hit the desk with a thud. His friend was watching us with interest, but both Matt and I ignored him. Probably because Matt didn't want to admit he knew me, and I didn't want to admit I didn't know his friend's name. "Maybe I wanted to sit in the front row and it was my bad luck that the only open seat was next to you."

"There are three open seats up here."

Obviously, it would have behooved me to notice that little fact before opening my mouth, huh? "Hey, if you're going to be my boyfriend, then I have to get used to being in your presence, don't I? I'm practicing."

"Boyfriend?" Matt's friend had his chair up on two legs, he was leaning so far over to hear our conversation. "Matt's your boyfriend?"

Matt shot me a truly lethal look.

As if that comment was my fault! He's the one who'd egged me on, giving me a hard time for sitting next to him, and he was going to benefit from this relationship too. "It's about the job, Matt."

"It better be."

He didn't have to spell out the "or else." I already knew: He'd expose my lie to everyone and completely humiliate me.

It was definitely time to work on my dad. What if he didn't have a job this summer?

No, he had to. *He had to.*

"Boyfriend?" His friend wasn't giving up.

Matt gave him a look. "None of your business."

"Sure it is. What about Liz?"

Oops. That girlfriend thing. Hoped he'd already explained the situation to her so she didn't hear about it from anyone else. Wouldn't want to add *that* to my list of things to apologize to him for.

Matt groaned and slid down in his chair. "I can't deal with this."

He looked so cute with his forehead all wrinkled and his mouth so unhappy, I almost wanted to hug him.

Well, not really, but he did make me feel a little warm and fuzzy toward him. Which was a good thing, I suppose, seeing as how I was going to have to convince more than a few people that we were dating.

Whoa.

I'd never had a boyfriend in my life. I had no idea how to act like someone's girlfriend. Matt would have to instruct me. Since he had a girlfriend already, he'd be able to clue me in.

Yeah, I was so sure he'd be glad to teach me girlfriend guidelines. Somehow I was one hundred percent convinced geometry was more his speed.

"Matt."

I looked up to find Blue standing in front of us. What now?

He glanced up, a pained look on his face. "What?"

"I invited you and Natalie to come out with me and my boyfriend, and she said she'd check with you. Has she checked? Are we on for Saturday night?"

No way was I going to let him catch my eye on that one. Instead, I looked out the window and admired the leaves that were just starting to turn color.

"Saturday night?" Matt's friend spoke up. "I thought you were coming to my house for a movie? You going to bring *her?*" He thumbed at me like I had cooties or something.

Yes, I felt wanted. "I told Blue that I thought you already had plans with your friend," I said, enunciating clearly just in case he was too mad to hear clearly. "I didn't commit to anything."

He groaned, leaned his head back and closed his eyes. I felt kinda sorry for him actually.

"Blue, please take your seat."

Saved by Ms. Olsen! Not that she was off my black list. After all, she was the cause of all my troubles. Her insistence that I have a tutor had landed me in this mess in the first place. Yes, it was all her fault.

I spent the rest of the class being mad at her. Actually, I spent the first five minutes being mad and imagining embarrassing things happening to her. At that point, Matt picked my pen up off my notebook, shoved it into my hand and glared at me. "Listen and take notes."

Right. Probably would be a good idea.

I actually took two pages of notes; the most ever. Whenever I started to daydream, I'd see Matt out of the corner of my eye writing furiously. It was like he was psychic, because every time, he'd look up and scowl at me. Got rid of my daydreaming without fail.

Who knew that being threatened was the key to improved concentration? That and the fact that I wasn't sitting next to Blue, so I had no one to pass notes to. Somehow I doubted Matt would be too psyched if I passed him a note about how Ms. Olsen's shirt didn't match her shoes at all.

Matt bolted from class two minutes early, so Saturday night was left undecided and I didn't know where to meet him for tutoring.

I chose not to chase after him, though. Go figure. Even I'm smarter than that.

Tomboy.

That's what I was.

My reflection in the girls' locker room did me no favors. I was about to see Zach, and I looked like a boy. Or at least not like the glam girl Allie always projected.

"You coming, Natalie?"

I grinned. "Sure thing, Val." I trotted out to the field with the gang, and we started stretching near the guys. Zach was there and he was checking me out, despite my lack of a cool haircut.

I ignored him and laughed at something Val said. If Matt showed up today, I'd kill him.

I was stretching my calves on the bottom step of the bleachers when I felt his presence.

Zach's, not Matt's.

He said nothing. Just climbed on the step next to me and stretched his calf.

Should I say something? Try to explain about the Matt thing? Be cool?

"You got a boyfriend, huh?"

My heart skipped, but I managed a restrained shrug. "Kinda."

"What does that mean?"

I eyed him, but he wasn't looking at me. He was gazing across the field at some random whatever in the distance. Yeah, he was trying to play it cool too. "It means kinda."

"Does it mean you have plans for Friday night? I'm having a party." He glanced at me. "Cross-country team members only, so your boyfriend can't come."

My sneaker slipped off the step and I crashed down and smacked my knee on the metal. Ow. "Friday night? A party? At your house?"

"Are you okay?"

I stopped rubbing my knee and stood up. "I'm fine."

"You need to take care of those legs."

Yeah, no kidding. I flexed my knee, then hopped up and down on it. "See? Fine."

He grinned. Nice teeth. Cute dimples. "So, how about Friday then?"

"Ah . . . What time?"

"Nine?"

"You're asking me?"

"Nine."

Dinner was at seven. I could probably get out by nine. "Yeah, I can make it."

He grinned. "Cool."

Understatement of the year.

"Need me to pick you up?"

I couldn't imagine it would go over well to have another boy show up to take me out when I was trying to convince my parents that Matt was my boyfriend. "No. If you can give me directions, I'll catch a ride." With whom?

I'd figure something out. No way was I going to miss the first and best social opportunity of my life for some family game night!

"Natalie! Let's go!" Valerie was waving at me.

"Is Valerie coming?"

"Of course."

Sweet. I was so in. At least until Sunday, when our next meet was. If I blew that, I was out again.

I met Matt on the front porch before he'd even had time to get off his bike. "Hi."

I was so nervous. He'd been completely not interested in discussing the boyfriend thing all week during our tutoring sessions. Mr. All Business. He'd said he'd be here tonight at seven, and that was it.

How was I supposed to act with a boyfriend? I had no idea. "How was the ride?"

He didn't even get off his bike. He just sat there with his helmet on. "I can't do this."

I nearly fell off the step in my rush to get down the stairs to grab his throat and kill him. "What?" I shoved my hands in my pockets when I got near him. Maybe he just couldn't do it tonight. Maybe he wasn't talking about the boyfriend thing in general.

"I spent two hours on the phone with Liz last night. She's not into it."

"You said she'd understand. That she'd think it was funny!"

"I was wrong." He rested one foot on a pedal and the other on the ground. "I can't do this to her."

"What's her problem? Doesn't she trust you?"

Matt narrowed his eyes. "One of her friends heard I had a new girlfriend and called her."

"Oh." This whole situation was getting way too complicated. "You couldn't buy her a necklace or something?"

"No."

"Why not?"

"Because it's not like that." He started to wheel his bike backwards. "I'll still be your tutor, and you don't have to tell people, but I'm going to deny the boyfriend thing."

"But . . ."

"No."

The front door swung open and my dad walked out onto the porch. Great. Matt's timing couldn't have been more perfect. Now he could witness my officially being kicked off the cross-country team. Quick, what's worse than being a stupid jock? A stupid jock without a sport or a team. I wouldn't have any group to belong to, not even my closest friends, who apparently had become a boyfriend clique.

"Welcome, Matt." My dad came off the steps and walked right out onto the pathway to shake his hand. "I'm really looking forward to dinner tonight. If you're interested and can drag yourself away from Natalie, I'd love to show you some projects I have going on at the moment."

Matt stopped rolling toward the street, and I saw the yearning in his eyes.

Go, Dad. "And Dad, isn't there a possibility you could hire him for the summer to do research?"

"Now, Natalie, let's not go promising anything yet. It would take an extraordinary sophomore to impress me enough to hire him for the summer." He lifted his brow at Matt and I saw the challenge in his gaze.

Matt hesitated, and his knee was jiggling. "What would the summer research be on?"

"Come on in and I'll show you."

Matt looked at me, then back at my dad. "I guess it couldn't hurt to come in."

"What are you talking about? We're the friendliest family around. Just ask Natalie." My dad grabbed the handlebars. "If you sit out here dithering, dinner will be ready and we won't have time to go through the projects in my office."

Matt lifted his chin. "Yes, sir." He swung his leg off his bike, and I knew he was hooked.

Score one for my dad.

Nine-fifteen. Valerie was due here any minute to pick me up for Zach's party, yet the Trivial Pursuit game was in high gear. It was Matt and me against my mom and dad. Matt and I were actually a good team, because I knew all the sports and entertainment and he rocked at everything else. The dude was smart, there was no getting around that. But at least I was able to answer *some* questions, so I wasn't a total idiot, right? I mean, Matt had to realize that I had somewhat of a functioning brain, even if I sucked at geometry.

Since my mom and dad were good too, it was the fastest game in the history of the Page household. We both had six pies and were going for the top.

And you know what? I was having fun. Matt was sitting next to me on the couch, and even though we weren't touching each other or anything, we were on the same team. It was nice not to be fighting with him all the time.

Put me in a great mood to go try to woo Zach.

"Um . . ." I glanced at my watch again. "I have to leave soon." I'd been hoping the night would end on its own and I could slip out, but it didn't look like that was going to happen. I had a feeling Matt and my parents would keep playing until two in the morning.

Everyone stopped laughing and stared at me. "Since when?" my mom asked.

"Team meeting."

"At nine on a Friday night?" My dad looked skeptical.

"Yeah, it's a varsity thing." I shifted nervously. "JV doesn't have them. Since I'm now a scoring runner, I have to go."

My mom frowned. "Well, it's good you're a scoring runner and everything . . ."

Be still my beating heart. How would I ever survive such endorsement? Made me swell with pride. "The girls' captain is picking me up."

Matt lifted a brow, and I could tell he didn't believe me. "This is for the entire team?" His accent on *entire* made it clear what he was asking. Would Zach be there?

"Yes." I eyed him. "But if you want to stay and hang out with my dad going over physics stuff, I'm sure that's fine with him. Probably good to get me out of the way so you don't need to entertain me."

Matt's gaze brightened and he glanced at my dad. "I could stay."

My dad clapped his hands. "Excellent."

No way had my dad ever looked that excited about spending a Friday night with me. Why couldn't I have had jock parents who actually appreciated how hard I worked at running, and how amazing it was that their sophomore daughter had scored second for the team last weekend?

But no. My dad cared about science and my mom cared about her businesses, which her daughter had shown no interest in. The only time we'd ever gone to one of her shops was when Allie had wanted to get her nails done. Their daughter wasn't a brain and didn't get into pampering herself.

A total waste of genetics, no doubt.

Add stupidity on top of it? They'd probably disown me.

A knock sounded at the door, and I jumped up. "That's probably Val. I'll see you guys."

My mom stood up. "We'll go meet this Val. How long has she been driving?"

"Mom . . ." I wailed. "Don't embarrass me."

She ignored me and marched to the door and pulled it open. "Hi, I'm Natalie's mother. Won't you come in for a bit and chat?"

Valerie was wearing a short skirt, a camisole and

had glittery blue eye shadow on. I suddenly felt very dowdy in my jeans and top. It was one of my cutest outfits, but looked like I'd pulled it out of a garbage can in comparison to Valerie's. Val smiled at my mom. "I'd love to, but we're already running late. Another time?"

My mom's eyes narrowed. "No. You'll come in."

I was going to die of embarrassment. "Mom. Coach is waiting. If we're late we won't get to run on Sunday." I shot Val a look, hoping she wouldn't blow my cover.

She gave me a wink. "Yes, Mrs. Page. Coach will bench us, and then we'll lose the meet and let our team down."

My mom frowned, and then my dad and Matt wandered out of the family room. Crud. I so didn't need Matt to show up. "Who's this?" my dad asked.

"Valerie Kranz." She stuck out her hand and flashed him a brilliant smile. "Team captain." Her gaze flicked toward Matt. "Are you her brother?"

"Boyfriend," my dad said, putting his arm around Matt's shoulder. "Smart kid."

Matt's face shuttered, but he didn't deny the boyfriend bit.

I almost wanted him to, when I saw the look of surprise and disdain on Valerie's face. Maybe having him as my boyfriend *wasn't* going to help me with Zach. Maybe he wasn't cool enough to make me look appealing. Maybe he was so uncool that he'd only drag me down.

Then I checked him out more closely. Yeah, he was still wearing the glasses and his shirt was a neatly ironed plaid oxford, but he had a nice smile and there was no way to miss those blue eyes. Plus he had a hot girlfriend.

Matt might be a geek, but he was definitely not a loser.

So I smiled at him. He didn't return it. "Can I have a word with you, Matt?"

Before he could say no, I grabbed his arm, detached him from my dad and dragged him into the family room and shut the door behind us. "So? What's the deal?"

He straightened his shirt. "What deal?"

"Boyfriend or not?"

His eyes glittered. "I want to work for your dad."

"Then it's a go?"

"I guess." He rubbed his forehead. "I have no idea how I'm going to handle this with Liz."

That wasn't my problem. I wondered if he'd be upset if I started dancing a victory dance? Didn't matter. No time. "What about tomorrow night then? Will you come to dinner with my friends?"

"Oh, come on, Natalie. Give me a break."

"If you don't, the boyfriend thing will never fly."

"Why can't you tell them the truth? They won't tell your parents, will they?"

I bit my lip. How to explain to an ultra-confident brainiac what it was like to feel like a loser who needed to prove herself? "Please?"

He looked toward the front hall, as if he could see my dad through the wooden door. Finally he shrugged. "Fine. But it can't be late because I need to go over to my friend's house afterwards."

No way was I going to take offense that he didn't invite me. So he was ashamed of me and didn't want his friends to know me? So what? It wasn't like we were really dating or anything. "It's not a problem. I can't stay out late because I have a meet on Sunday. Meet me here at five-thirty and we'll do an early dinner. Then you can go do your thing." Without me. Jerk. "You know, you owe me an apology."

"For what?"

"For calling me a snob."

"You didn't know my name."

"Yeah, well, I'm not ashamed to take you out to meet my friends."

A look of surprise flitted across his face, like he hadn't thought of that.

"You, on the other hand, can make no such claim."

His mouth dropped open. "You *want* to hang out with my friends?"

I tried to look haughty. "I could care less. I was simply pointing out that you're the snob, not me."

"I'm not a snob."

"No? Then why do you call me a jock like it's a bad thing?"

"You call me a brain!"

"And then I invite you out with my friends. Big difference." I pulled open the door. "See you tomorrow."

By the time I reached the front hall, Val had wooed my parents and we were excused. To go hang with Zach.

Matt didn't come back into the front hall to see me off. Good. I hoped he was feeling bad. Just because he was smart didn't mean he was better than me.

7

Valerie gave me a high five on the way to the car. "Lying to your parents? Nice. The team meeting was a great call."

"Yeah." It was weird to be complimented for lying to my parents. I hadn't really thought of it as a lie either, except for the part about Coach Thompson being there. I mean, Zach had made it clear that it was a party for the team only. Party/meeting. What was the difference? It was bonding with the team.

Five other girls were in the car already, so I ended up sharing the far backseat in the Suburban with a girl I didn't know. Didn't even recognize actually. She ignored me and everyone chatted about people I didn't know, so I spent the ride over looking out the window and counting mailboxes. And wishing my friends were there with me.

I was the last one out of the SUV at Zach's house, and I had to run to catch up to the rest of the girls. No way was I walking in there by myself.

The door was open and music was blaring, and there were a lot of cars in the driveway and on the street in front of the house. When I stepped inside, I knew Zach had lied.

There were tons of kids I didn't know. Kids who weren't on our team, and who definitely weren't runners.

"Hi, guys." Zach swung in front of us, emerging out of the crowd. "Welcome." He shot me a special smile. "Hey, Natalie. Glad you could make it."

Val shot me a questioning look, but she was dragged off by her friends before I could ask her what was wrong.

They left me and Zach in the foyer together, along with a bunch of other kids wandering through, but Zach was the only one I knew. In fact, I didn't see any other kids from the team there. "Want a drink?"

"Water is fine." There were kids drinking beer, but there was no way I was doing that. My running was too important to mess with.

Zach took my hand and guided me back through the crowd toward the kitchen, past Valerie who gave me another look that definitely wasn't altogether friendly. What was up with that? It wasn't my fault Zach had grabbed me; not that I was fighting it. I did have a question for him, though, and I'd ask it as soon as he slowed down.

The hallway was packed with kids, and I saw one guy from our team. He gave me a nod, which made me all warm and gooey inside. I was beginning to be noticed.

"Here." Zach pulled a bottle of water out of the fridge and handed it to me.

"Thanks." Someone bumped me just as I got the lid off, and I dumped half the bottle on Zach. "Sorry."

He frowned, but didn't say anything as he wiped off the water.

"Um, Zach?"

"Yeah?"

"You said this party was for team members only."

He grinned and tossed the soggy paper towel in the sink. "I said that so you wouldn't bring your boyfriend."

Whoa. "Really?"

"Yeah." He touched my arm. "He didn't seem like he'd fit in with this crowd."

Double whoa. Was he hitting on me? Even though I had a boyfriend? Apparently, yes, seeing as how he had lied to me to make sure Matt wouldn't show up.

I was totally floored. Zach was actually thinking he had to work to get me? Me? Hah! I was all his!

"Some of us were planning to watch a movie in the family room. Interested?"

Be cool. "What movie?"

"You can pick from my DVD collection. As the newest team member, it's your special privilege." He tucked his hand beneath my elbow and guided me out of the kitchen. "Make sure you keep that water away from me. You're deadly with it."

I chuckled. "You aren't mad?"

"No, but I'll get you back at some point, I promise."

Should I tell him that I was looking forward to that?

We walked into the family room to see Valerie and her friends spread out over the couches, along with most of the guys from the team, plus a few other kids I didn't know. Maybe ten altogether.

This time, there was no mistaking the coolness in Valerie's gaze. She stood up immediately when she saw me and made her way over to us. "I have to go to the bathroom. Keep me company?"

"Um . . ." I glanced at Zach.

"She's going to pick out the movie," he said. "You know where the bathroom is, Val."

"Pick out your own movie." Valerie took my arm. "Come on, sophomore girl."

If she took me out into a dark alley, I was going to run for it before she could whip out a gun and blow me away. But she stopped in the hallway right outside the room, and turned me to face her. "We need to talk."

Apparently. "What's up?"

"Stay away from Zach."

"Why?"

"Because he's no good."

"At what?" From the look on her face, I'd guess she wasn't all that high on my flippant response.

"He always likes to hook up with the new girls on the team, and then he dumps them."

My heart sank. "Really?"

"Yes. I'm telling you this only to protect you."

"But . . ."

"If he messes with you, and you go around getting all

depressed, then your running will suffer. This is my last season, and I want to be state champs, and to do that, we need you, not a sniveling shell of Zach's leftovers."

Yeesh. Could she sound any more hostile? I mean, I wanted to win too, but I hoped I didn't sound like that. "My running is fine."

Valerie leaned closer and put her hands on my shoulders. "Trust me. Stay away from him. He's bad news for girls like you."

Well, that totally sucked, because I'd really liked him. He seemed too nice to only be interested in me so he could dump me.

Val put her arm around me. "Don't look so sad. We'll find you someone else."

"I'm not sad." I lifted my chin. "I have a boyfriend anyway, so it doesn't matter." Was I enjoying this boyfriend thing too much? *Must remember it's not true*. It did feel good to be able to say it, though.

We walked back into the room, and Val dropped her arm and veered off to sit in the empty seat next to Zach. She flashed me a knowing look that clearly conveyed she'd done that to protect me from myself, so I didn't sit next to him despite her warning.

Whatever. I flopped down on an empty couch and folded my arms across my chest. Yeah, this party was turning out to be fun.

Elaine O'Neill, the slowest runner on our team even though she was a senior, sat down next to me just as the movie started. "What did Val say to you?" She kept her voice low.

I shrugged and watched the television. "Nothing." As if I'd admit I'd almost been fooled by Zach.

"Did you know that she used to date Zach?"

My head spun toward her of its own accord. "When?"

"For two years. He dumped her over the summer."

"*Two years?*" *Two years?* How could he be running around using the new girls on the team if he'd had a girlfriend the whole time?

"I noticed that Zach has been checking you out. I think he's interested in you."

My stomach tightened, but I said nothing.

"Val has noticed too, and she's not going to let that happen." She lowered her voice. "Normally, she'd warn you off and make your life miserable, but you're too good of a runner. She has to be nice to you, because she wants to win state too badly to risk messing with you."

I felt sick. Who was I supposed to believe?

"Zach's a nice guy. Too nice for her. If you like him, don't let her stop you." Elaine patted my arm. "She can't touch you as long as you keep running fast."

"Why are you telling me this?"

"Because she's only nice to the fast runners."

And Elaine wasn't fast. They'd probably never used her score in the entire time she'd been on the team. Which meant that Val hadn't been nice to her and this was her payback opportunity.

Or maybe Elaine hated me because I was a sophomore and beating her. Or maybe Zach really *was* a jerk, but Val still liked him, and Elaine didn't care if I got hurt as long as Val did too?

Who could I trust?

Zach got up and left the room, and Elaine winked at me. "That's an excuse to get away from Val. When he comes back, he'll sit next to you. If you like him, don't let Val scare you off." Then she moved to a nearby armchair and left me alone on the couch.

I pulled my knees against my chest and tried to watch the movie. And Val. She was still sitting next to Zach's empty seat, a look of smug contentment on her face. Because she'd foiled Zach's attempt to destroy me, or my attempts to win over the boy she still wanted?

Zach walked back into the room with a soda in his hand and my belly got all jiggly. Was he a letch who I didn't want near me? Or was he a great guy who deserved all my love?

He studied Val for a sec, then looked my way. Still undecided, I avoided his gaze and focused on the movie, as if I had no idea what was going on. Out of the corner of my eye, I saw him move . . . in my direction!

The couch shifted under his weight and then was still.

I didn't dare breathe. Or look at him. Or at Val.

"Enjoying the movie?" His breath was warm on my ear, and I jumped, accidentally elbowing him in the throat.

He inhaled and gagged and grabbed his neck.

"Oh, geez. I'm sorry. I really didn't mean to do that." I was such an idiot. "You startled me."

I heard someone laughing, and I looked over at Val. Sure enough, she watching us and giggling. Because I'd made a fool of myself with Zach, or because Zach the jerk had gotten what he deserved?

Elaine gave me a sympathetic smile, but I didn't respond. Who was the one lying to me?

I ignored all of them and turned back to Zach, who was breathing much more quietly now. "Want some water?"

"No." He took a few more deep breaths, his hand still rubbing his neck. "You've dumped water on me, sat down on the other side of the room from me and tried to kill me. Should I be taking a hint?"

Amazed, I almost laughed. "You're not mad at me?"

"Scared of you, yes. Mad? No."

This time, I did laugh. "I'm really sorry. I . . . you make me nervous."

He lifted a brow. "Why?"

Probably too soon to tell him that it was because I totally loved him and because I wasn't sure whether he was a lying, deceitful snake. "I don't know."

He lifted his chin and exposed his neck to me. "Is there a mark?"

"Actually, there's a little red spot about the size of my elbow."

"Where?"

I touched the front of his neck really lightly.

"There."

He flinched and I jumped. Then he laughed. "Got you."

"Jerk." Said with a soppy grin. He was cute, and funny, and he wasn't holding a grudge.

No way was he a jerk.

Or was he? He had lied about the party being for the team only, but that was because he liked me. That was excusable, wasn't it? I mean, no guy had ever pursued me before. It didn't seem wise to question his motives too closely, especially since I liked him!

Matt showed up at my front door at exactly five-thirty on Saturday night. He was wearing his usual outfit and had the strap around his jeans to keep them from being caught in his bike chain.

No way could he hold a candle to Zach.

Zach, who had sat next to me all night and never tried to make a move on me. He'd even given me a ride home when I'd had to leave before Valerie was ready, thanks to my curfew. No make-out attempt in the car either. That meant one of two things: Either he didn't like me in a potential-girlfriend kind of way at all, in which case I'd have to spend the next month crying alone in my room, or else it meant that he did like me that way, but he was so the opposite of what Valerie had said.

I preferred the latter scenario, but would it ruin my chances to be in with Valerie and her crowd? Who had more power over my social life, Valerie or Zach?

"You ready?"

I blinked and remembered Matt was standing in front of me. "Yeah. Don't I look ready?"

He shrugged. "I kinda figured you to be the type to dress up for a date." He lifted a brow behind his glasses. "Seeing as how this is a date, right? Or was I wrong?"

My hands went to my hair. "You don't think I look okay?"

"Do you care what I think?"

"Well, I should practice."

"Practice for what?"

"A real date." Yeesh. Wasn't he listening?

Matt frowned. "You've never had a real date?"

"Not all of us have pictures in our wallets of beautiful people declaring their undying love."

He grinned. "She is pretty, isn't she?"

I frowned. "Is that why you're embarrassed to have me meet your friends? Because I'm not pretty enough? I figured it was only that I was too stupid, but I didn't really think of the looks thing. But there's that too, isn't there?"

Matt stared at me. "Are you serious?"

"Yeah."

"I have a girlfriend. That's why I don't want to bring you around."

"I *know* that. But it's more than that, isn't it?" I opened the front door and beckoned him to bring the bike in, my mind flirting with a new idea. "Can you teach me how to be girlfriend material?"

He kept the bike between me and him, giving me a wide berth like I was some crazed fool who was going to come after him. "I thought this was only dinner with your friends."

"Yeah, but why can't we make it a training session too?"

He leaned the bike against the couch in the den, then he turned to me. "Natalie, I really don't want to get involved in your life. I'm your tutor and . . ."

I jumped at him and slapped my hand over his mouth. "Shut up! My parents are upstairs." His breath was warm on my hand, and for a minute, we stood there like that.

Then he put his hand around my wrist and pulled my hand away. "Sorry."

I was so close to him that I could smell his aftershave or cologne or whatever it was again. So faint, but yummy. I had no idea a guy could smell so good. I cleared my throat and took a step back. "We have to convince my friends we're dating, but I have no idea how I'm supposed to act with a boyfriend. I mean, do we have to make out and stuff?"

He looked horrified. "No!"

"Thanks for that ego boost." I waved him off when he was about to launch into his girlfriend speech again. Yeah, the girlfriend would have accounted for a gentle rebuff, not the look of utter disgust and terror on his face at the thought of making out with me. "I didn't want to make out. I was trying to figure out the plan for tonight. You know, how to behave." I held out my arms and stood for inspection. "You think I'm not dressed for a date, huh?"

"It's fine. I just thought you were the type to . . . you know . . . do something different." His cheeks were bright red and he looked mortally embarrassed. "Can we go?"

I walked over to the mirror in the front hall and inspected myself. Cute jeans that were tight across the butt, a shirt that showed off what little boobs I had and I'd blown dry my hair and put on makeup. What else was I supposed to do?

Matt appeared behind me, peering over my head into the mirror. His shoulders were about five inches higher than mine. How could he be that tall? He didn't seem to be a big guy. But he definitely was. A geek who was tall, knew how to kiss and had a hot girlfriend. Who'd have thought? Not that he could compare to Zach, but it did raise some interesting possibilities for the future. Maybe I should join the Physics Club.

Or not. No need to showcase my intellectual shortcomings to people who valued that stuff. I was sure I'd be as good—or rather, as bad—at physics as I was at geometry.

The doorbell rang, and he moved away from me. Darn it. I'd kind of liked him standing next to me.

Whatever.

I opened the door to find Blue standing on my doorstep. Colin was our ride, since I wasn't too stoked about riding on Matt's handlebars to the restaurant. "Blue, this is Matt Turner. Matt, this is Blue Waller."

Matt nodded. "I know who you are."

"And I know who you are." Blue clapped her hands. "Well, let's go. I'm starved!"

Right. I'd forgotten that they were both in my geometry class. Blue had even asked Matt about coming tonight. Note to self: Plug in brain.

Matt followed me to the car and exchanged greetings with Colin. He slipped into the backseat with me and then leaned over once Colin was driving. "How old is Colin?" His voice was low and tense.

"He's a freshman at Harvard."

Matt swore under his breath and leaned back in his seat. His jaw was tense and a muscle was twitching in his neck.

"What's wrong?" I scooted closer to him so Blue wouldn't hear me over the music in the front.

"Nothing."

"I don't believe you."

He shot a glance at me. "Nothing."

"Are you intimidated because he's in college?"

"No."

"Because he's really a nice guy. And Blue's our age, so it's not like he hates hanging out with sophomores."

"I'm fine." But he looked a little more relaxed.

I patted his arm. "Good." Wonder what he'd think of Theo, who was also in college but who was a major jock. According to Frances he'd bulked up now that he was playing college football. I hadn't seen Theo in a couple months, but even with his high school bod, Matt would have seen him as too athletic.

Probably should have thought of that before agreeing to tonight. It would be mucho awkward if Matt started shooting his anti-jock hostility toward Theo. "Um . . . Matt?"

"Yeah?"

I leaned closer. Did he smell good or what? Maybe I should whisper things to him all night so I had to get close enough for a dose of Matt's aura. "Do you remember Theo Waller? He graduated this past year?"

Matt eyed me warily. "Yeah."

"He's coming tonight."

His eyes narrowed. "Nice."

"Oh, come on. He's totally nice. Get over your jock complex, will you?"

"I don't have a jock complex."

"No? Then how come you're always judging me just because I run?"

"You judge me because I'm smart."

"But I don't hate you. I'd be willing to hang out with your friends."

"I doubt that."

"I would!"

His eyes flashed. "Then come with me tonight."

"Tonight?" My gut sank. "But I have to be home early for my meet tomorrow."

"Convenient."

"Yeah, because you already know I have to get home early. You don't want me to come. You don't want to hang with my friends and you don't want me near yours." I bit my lip. The truth hurt, even if I pretended it didn't. Sure, Matt and his friends were brainiac geeks, but I still didn't want them to think I was a loser, too.

He narrowed his eyes. "Fine. Sunday night. Study group at my place."

I swallowed. "Study group?" That would showcase my talents. Not.

His gaze softened a hair. "We won't do math, okay?"

"Um . . ."

He got this smug grin on his face, like he knew I was going to come up with an excuse not to hang with his friends. Was that why he'd invited me? To prove that I was a snob? Forget it. He had another thing coming. "Sure. I'll come."

His grin faded. "You will?"

"Yeah." I folded my arms across my chest. "Which means you have to be nice to Theo tonight. How you treat Theo is how I'll treat your friends." Oh, that was a good one. I was pretty impressed with myself on that one.

Matt scowled. "Fine."

"Fine."

Blue looked back at us. "Are you two done arguing? Because if you are, we're here."

I looked out the window. "You picked Italian?"

"Your favorite pasta place. We know how you like your pasta on the night before races. You runners are so predictable."

Matt rolled his eyes and I stuck my tongue out at him and climbed out of the car. Nearly smashed my door into the side of the Jeep that was parked next to us.

A Jeep very similar to one driven by a certain hot cross-country team captain. I frowned and peered into the backseat. A sweatshirt with Mapleville Cross Country across the front was lying on the floor.

Holy cow. Zach was here? And I was here with my "boyfriend"?

Crud.

8

When we stepped inside, I nervously scanned the foyer for Zach, but there was no sign of him. Good. Maybe it wasn't his Jeep. *Yeah, Natalie. Wishful thinking.* Okay, so maybe he would be seated in another part of the restaurant. More chance of that.

Blue elbowed me. "There's Frances and Allie."

They were seated at the back of the room at a long table. And I didn't see Zach anywhere between us and them. Score.

I hunched behind Matt, using him as a shield in case Zach was around, and followed him through the maze of tables, ignoring the questioning look he shot over his shoulder at me. No need for him to know every warped thing that went on in my mind, was there? Definitely not.

Theo and Colin were already sitting across from each other, talking about college, and Blue and Frances were sitting on the end, next to the boys. That left the other side of the table for us young 'uns. Matt sat on the end, so I sat next to him, across from Allie. Tad was across from Matt, so that was good. Tad was a sophomore . . . except he was a runner too. Where did all the athletes come from? I felt really self-conscious. But Tad was cool, so Matt should feel fine.

Greetings went all around, and I saw Matt's gaze flicker when he was introduced to Theo, who had definitely gotten more muscular. After the initial intro, everyone sat back down and I swear every guy's arm went up across the back of his girlfriend's chair.

Except me and Matt.

Hmm . . . awkward much?

"So, Matt, where do you go to school?" Tad asked. Nice, friendly guy. I could see why Allie liked him.

"Mapleville." Matt nodded at me. "With Natalie."

"Really? You run for them too?"

I felt like kicking Tad under the table.

"No." Matt took a long drag of his water.

"Soccer, then?"

His jaw flexed. "No."

I leaned over and rested my chin on Matt's shoulder. "I'd never want to date another athlete," I said to Tad. "That's who I hang with all day, and I like dating someone who has something else to talk about." I could tell Matt was uncomfortable, and it was my fault for putting him in this situation.

Matt glanced at me, which meant his face was about a quarter of an inch from mine, seeing as how I was still using his shoulder for a pillow. I'd meant it as an expression of solidarity, but now I was sort of enjoying it. It felt good. I don't know why, but it did. So I smiled at him.

He smiled back. Nice teeth. Hadn't realized how white and straight they were. "Did you have braces?" I asked.

"Nope."

"Lucky dog." I'd just gotten my braces off about six months ago. It was so great not to be carrying around a wad of wax anymore.

"I agree," Tad said.

We both looked at Tad. Had Matt also forgotten there were others at the table?

Tad was nodding, and rubbing Allie's shoulder. "I like that Allie and I have stuff to talk about besides running." He smiled at her. "I'm glad you come to my meets, though."

She grinned back. "I know enough to realize that when you win it's a good thing."

"You've figured out a lot more than that. I appreciate it."

Ugh. Sickening.

I tried to catch Matt's gaze to trade vomit expressions, but he was staring at Tad and Allie with a wistful look on his face that caught my gut and wrenched it. Was he thinking of Liz? Missing her? Wishing she was around so he could whisper disgusting nothings into her ear while others grew ill listening?

Tad looked at Matt. "Are you coming to the meet tomorrow?"

"Tomorrow?"

"Yeah. It's a big meet."

"I'm going," Allie chirped up. "Double benefit. I get to watch Tad and Natalie." She nodded at me. "Do you realize Natalie is almost the best runner on the team, and she's beating juniors and seniors? They love her."

My cheeks felt hot. "Matt doesn't care about that."

"Why not? He should." Allie eyed Matt accusingly. "Why don't you care? Just because you don't run doesn't mean you shouldn't care about her running."

"Allie! Shut up!" I tried to kick her, but just smashed my toe into the table leg. Stupid! If I broke my toe I'd have a heck of a time racing tomorrow. I bit my lip and tried to will the pain away. "Leave him alone."

Matt shifted next to me. "I care about her running."

"Then why does she think you don't?"

"Allie! What's your problem?"

She didn't take her eyes off Matt. "Why does she think you don't?"

Matt glanced at me. "Um . . . I don't know."

The poor guy. I so owed him.

"So then come to the race tomorrow and show you care."

"He has to work," I blurted out. "He can't make it."

He gave me an odd look, and I couldn't tell if he was glad I'd make an excuse for him. "Would you want me to come?"

"Of course she does," Allie said. "Doesn't she, Tad?"

"I like it when Allie comes," Tad said. "I can't speak for Natalie."

Matt ignored them. "Would you want me to come?"

Did he mean, would I want a real boyfriend to come, or would I want him in particular to come? What was he asking me? "Do you want to come?"

"You guys are pathetic," Allie announced.

"Hey, Natalie."

My head whipped up so fast I thought my neck was going to snap. Zach was standing at the end of the table, between Tad and Matt. OMG. "Hi."

Matt twisted around to check out Zach, then he shot me a questioning look.

Great. So he remembered who Zach was. I wasn't sure whether that was a good thing or a horrible thing. I couldn't really think, my heart was beating so fast. Zach looked totally cute in a pair of ripped jeans and a loose T-shirt. I could see his biceps peeking out from under his sleeves—those wiry, ripped muscles that runners had, not the huge bulky ones like Theo.

Tad stuck out his hand. "Tad Simmons. I run for Medfield."

Zach shook it. "Zach Fulton. I'm captain of the Mapleville team."

Matt snorted under his breath and put his arm across the back of my chair. *Now* he does it? Did he think he was helping my cause or something?

Zach's eyes flickered over Matt's arm, then up to his face. "You're the boyfriend?"

"Yep."

Never heard Matt acknowledge the boyfriend status thing so emphatically. Interesting.

"How long have you guys been dating?"

"Long enough," Matt said. His arm slipped off the back of my chair and rested on my shoulders.

Long enough for what?

Zach looked at me. "Doesn't sound like it to me. Nat and I had fun at the party last night."

OMG. He'd totally made it sound like we'd been up to something.

Matt's arm tightened around my shoulders. "You mean the team thing?"

Zach winked at me. "Yeah, the *team* thing." His emphasis on the word team made it totally clear that it hadn't been a team thing at all.

Matt's fingers were digging into my shoulder so hard it almost hurt.

"We have an extra seat at our table," Zach said. "It would be nice to do some team bonding before the race. Talk strategy. It'll be good for you."

He wanted me to join him for dinner? Wow.

"She's fine here." Allie's voice was like ice. Frigid. "We're perfectly capable of prepping her for the race. Her *boyfriend* is her best inspiration."

Zach shrugged and smiled at me again. "If you change your mind, we're right over there." He pointed to a big booth in the corner. Valerie was sitting in it, along with a few other kids from the team. All seniors.

No one was paying us any attention, except for Valerie, who looked really pissed.

"Um . . . okay. Thanks for the invite."

"Good-bye," Allie said pointedly.

Zach gave me a final smile that curled my toes, then he glided away from the table.

Was he cool or what?

"What a complete scumbag," Allie spat out.

Tad nodded. "No kidding." He nodded at Matt. "I think you better plan on showing up tomorrow."

What? What was wrong with Zach?

Allie must have read the expression on my face. "He was hitting on you in front of your boyfriend! As if Matt wasn't even there. As if he could take you away from Matt anytime he wanted." She shook her head. "Disgusting. I hope he breaks an ankle in the race tomorrow."

"Allie!"

Tad was looking at me. "What team party last night?" He shot Matt a look of sympathy.

"Nothing happened with him," I blurted out. "He just made it sound that way." I looked at Matt. "I swear, Matt. He told me it was for team people only and then when I showed up all these other people were there. . . ." My voice faded as I recalled Zach had told me that no one else was allowed so I wouldn't bring my boyfriend. "I didn't realize it was a party, and I swear nothing happened. A bunch of us watched a movie, and that was it." Sure, we weren't actually dating, but I didn't want Matt or anyone else at the table to think I'd cheat on him.

Besides, Matt deserved better than that.

Matt stared at me for a long time. "I don't enjoy being jerked around."

"I know that! I didn't do anything!"

His gaze flicked toward Zach, who was watching us with a smug look on his face while Val leaned against him. "I don't like him enough to let him think he's better than me."

"He already does," Tad said. "Look at that expression on his face. He gives runners a bad name."

Matt locked his gaze on mine. "I have my pride."

I swallowed at the intense look on his face. Matt might be a brainiac, but there was nothing wimpy about the look on his face right now. He was pissed, and he was insulted.

"Is he still watching?" Matt asked.

I glanced at the table. "Yeah." Still sporting that smug look on his face too. Even though he was totally cute, it really did make him look like a jerk.

"Then let's give him something to watch." He curved his fingers around the back of my neck and applied gentle pressure. "Come here."

Oh my God. This wasn't going to be like the kiss at the field the other day. This was going to be the real thing.

My heart started pounding and I couldn't catch my breath.

When his lips touched mine, I was sure I was going to faint. They were so soft and warm and begging me to join them. So I kissed him back. I mean, I tried. I wasn't exactly the expert, but I tried to copy what he was doing. Well, I tried for a little bit; after that, I couldn't think. All I could do was taste his lips and feel his breath and try not to fall off my chair.

He finally pulled away, but not very far. His eyes were all smoky and made me all warm. "Apparently, running isn't the only thing you're good at." His voice was husky and gravelly and it made my skin pop up in goose bumps. He brushed his thumb over my lips, and I thought for sure I was going to die right on the spot.

"You, too." Was that my voice? Sounded awfully breathless.

The corner of his mouth curved up. "I'm not good at running."

"Well, you're good at kissing."

He broke into a full grin. "Thanks."

"I think that did it," Allie's voice broke into our magic bubble. "Zach's looking pissed, not smug."

Zach. I'd totally forgotten the kiss had been for him. Matt dropped his hand and turned away.

Total loss. I wanted him back. I wanted him to kiss me like that again. And again. And again. At the very least, I wanted him to kiss me until I actually did fall off my chair. Not that it would take much.

"Your hands are shaking." Allie pointed at my water

glass, which I'd picked up in an attempt to distract myself. "That must have been some kiss."

Matt and I both looked at my hand, which was very clearly trembling. The water was shivering, and the ice was clinking. I felt my cheeks heat up, and I couldn't look at him.

How totally embarrassing!

Matt said nothing, but he put his arm over the back of my chair and left it there until the food arrived.

"Is Matt here?"

I looked up from my stretch. "Hi, Allie. I haven't seen him." And I'd been looking, since the first minute we'd arrived at the meet. Not that I really thought he'd come, but I'd been sort of hoping after that kiss last night.

Yeah, sports weren't his thing.

Yeah, he wasn't actually my boyfriend.

But I'd been hoping that his ego would have made him come just to piss Zach off.

No such luck.

I hadn't even seen Zach except from a distance. The girls' race was first, so we were together and the boys were off somewhere warming up.

"Have you seen Tad?"

"No." I bent back over my leg and concentrated on my hamstring muscle. I'd sat down away from the rest of the girls, afraid of Val and her friends. Even Elaine, who said Val hated her, was stretching with those girls. I didn't know who was my friend and who wasn't.

Except for Allie. She was my friend.

"I'm going to go find Tad. I'll be back for your race." She pulled on my pigtail. "Good luck."

"Thanks." I needed it. Val wouldn't even look at me. The only way I was going to be back in that group was if I ran well. Nothing like pressure.

Which was fine. I could totally handle it.

The ten-minute warning came over the loudspeaker and I looked around again for Matt.

Nowhere.

So I stood up and shook out my legs.

"How are you feeling, sophomore girl?" Val was standing next to me suddenly.

"Good."

"You going to run fast?" There was a challenge in her gaze.

I met it. "Yes."

She nodded. "Is your boyfriend here?"

"No."

"Next time, tell him to come."

Where did that come from? "Why?"

"Because Zach was talking smack about you last night. He made a bet with the rest of the table that he could get you to cheat on your boyfriend and then he'd dump you."

My gut plummeted. "He did?"

She patted my shoulder. "Don't look so upset. I warned you what he was like."

I swallowed. Was that why he'd looked smug? Because he'd been making bets about me?

Elaine came up and stood next to Val. "Hi, Natalie."

"Hi." I made a pretense of tying my shoe, because I didn't know who to look at. Which one of them was lying to me?

"Hey, Natalie!"

The three of us spun around to find the boys running by us, Zach in the middle of the bunch. "Good luck, Nat!" He gave me a thumbs up as the group moved past us. Didn't even give Val and Elaine so much as a nod.

Elaine and Val turned back to me. Elaine gave me a soft smile, and Val glared at me. "If you make our team lose because you get tangled up with him and mess yourself up, I will be very pissed." She bent closer. "Stay away from him."

The five-minute warning came over the loudspeaker, and Elaine elbowed Val. "You're freaking her out right before the race, Val. If you want her to win, you're not doing it the right way."

Val blinked, then she smiled at me and slipped her arm around my shoulder. "You'll be great, Natalie. Don't let the other girls in the race rattle you by starting fast. Keep at your pace and then finish strong. They won't be able to keep it up." She kept up her stream of advice and warm tone as she herded me toward the starting line.

By the time I got there, my mind was spinning. I couldn't think, had no idea what my plan was and needed everyone to leave me alone so I could focus. And I had about two minutes to do so.

I shrugged off Val's arm. "Thanks for the advice. Good luck."

She nodded and moved off to her start position. I shook out my legs and tried to focus on the race, on my body, and tried to center my mind. But I kept thinking about Zach and Matt and Val and Elaine.

No! Focus!

The gun went off while I was still attempting to focus.

9

When I got home from the meet, my dad met me and my mom at the door. "How'd it go?"

I ignored him and walked inside, while I heard my mom whisper to him. Why whisper? As if I didn't know that I'd totally sucked. Our team had come in fifth in a meet that we could have won, because their new number two runner (that would be me) had come in sixth for the team. Since only the top five runners score, I didn't even count. But the worst part was that my horrific showing meant our usual sixth runner ended up fifth, so she was scored, and she ran so slow that having to use her score totally killed the team. None of the girls talked to me afterwards, except for Allie.

The only good thing was that it had been a nearby meet, so I'd gone home with my mom instead of on the team bus.

I threw my bag on the kitchen floor and yanked open the cabinet. Screw being fit. I was going for the cookies. Didn't matter what kind we had. I was eating them.

My dad walked into the kitchen and patted me on the shoulder. "Tough day, huh?"

"Can we not talk about it?" I carried the box of cookies to the table and opened them. Chocolate chip. Good. I shoved one in my mouth. "I'm going over to Matt's tonight to study with his friends."

He sat down across from me. "Sorry, Natalie, but Matt called. He can't make it tonight."

I stopped chewing. "What?"

"He said he'd meet you here tomorrow night at seven, though."

That was for our usual tutoring session. What about hanging with his friends?

Apparently, he'd concluded that wasn't going to happen, and I really couldn't figure out a way to take it that wasn't insulting and offensive.

"You okay, Nat?"

"Great." I took another bite of cookie, which now tasted like sawdust. "Just great."

By the time Matt showed up at my house on Monday night, I was so stressed I half expected to burst out in a major attack of zits at any second. School had *sucked*. Matt had avoided me in class, Val and the rest of the team had totally ignored me and I hadn't seen Zach to evaluate how he was feeling. And Blue had been whining all morning about how much she missed Colin until I was ready to push her into a trash can.

At this point, I'd take being used by Zach if it meant someone would say something nice to me.

I was already working on my geometry homework when Matt showed up. I let my dad answer the door and didn't even bother to go out and greet him. Let Matt suck up to my dad. I didn't care.

It took almost forty-five minutes for Matt to finish groveling. Then he came into the kitchen, dropped his bag on the table and said, "Ready to study?"

"Why did you blow me off last night?" Darn it! I'd totally resolved not to ask and not to care. I growled to myself and buried my nose in my homework. *Don't look at him.*

I felt him sit down next to me, but I didn't look up.

"How'd your race go?"

"Sucked."

"Really? Why?"

"Because I ran slow." Duh.

"Was Zach harassing you? Is that why?"

I finally looked up, and immediately wished I hadn't. He had taken off his glasses to clean them, and was looking at me through the bluest, most beautiful eyes I'd ever seen. Sure, I'd noticed they were blue and I'd thought they were nice, but without his glasses . . . wow.

He finished polishing his glasses and put them back on. "Well? Was Zach bugging you?"

I sat back in my chair. "Since when do you care?"

He opened his mouth, then snapped his lips shut. After a minute, he shifted. "We need to talk."

My gut plummeted. "About what?"

"Liz is really pissed."

"Your girlfriend? About what?"

"The fact that I kissed you on Saturday."

Coulda knocked me off the chair with a feather I was so surprised. "You told her?"

He frowned. "Of course I did. I'm not going to lie to her." He sighed. "She's not okay with our relationship anymore. The boyfriend status thing is making her uncomfortable." He cleared his throat. "She thinks I'm making up the tutoring thing as an excuse to hang out with you." He flicked his pen and wouldn't look at me. "She thinks I like you, and she's not happy."

Oh, wow. I was floored. The first question on my lips was to ask whether she was right, whether he did like me, but given the expression of misery on his face, I decided not to.

He looked up. "So, I promised to go to London and visit her over Thanksgiving, and the boyfriend thing has to stop. Except for your parents. We can study here, and keep up the charade with them, but no more public viewings."

I leaned back in my chair. "That's why you cancelled on me last night? Because Liz said so?" He was going to London to visit her? To visit his girlfriend? The one who loves him? The one who he is so good to that he won't lie to her about anything? That one?

"Yeah." He kept flicking his pen. "Sorry about that."

I chewed my lower lip and tried not to feel bummed, but I was. I totally was. I mean, *really* bummed. Like, stomach-hurting bummed.

"Natalie? You okay?"

I lifted my chin and smiled at him. "Fine. That's probably best. I don't want to push Zach away too much."

His face darkened. "I don't think you should date him."

"Why not?"

"Because."

"What kind of reason is that?"

He scowled at me. "I don't think he'd treat you well."

"Because he was flirting with me in front of you? So what? He likes me and he's not afraid to admit it." Or he *did* like me. After my horrible performance yesterday, I wasn't so sure where I stood.

"It's more than that."

"What is it?"

He shrugged. "Do what you want. It's not my problem."

"That's right." I sighed. It wasn't his problem, because he wasn't my boyfriend. Friend only. We were friends? Maybe. So why did that make me feel so bad? Because I didn't want another guy friend, not because I wanted him as anything more.

Yeesh. Can you imagine? Matt as my boyfriend? The cute eyes and nice smile would never make up for the fact he thought discussions about physics were interesting.

The kissing might, though. Ack! Stop thinking about that!

"Why are you blushing?"

"I'm not!" Heaven help me if he knew I'd really enjoyed that kiss. Wait a sec. Had I? Really enjoyed it?

There was no doubt. But it was only because he was a great kisser, right? Not because I *liked* him or anything? I mean, he was a brainiac jock-hater who was in love with his girlfriend. Three strikes. I held up my book. "Let's study."

"Yeah. Big test on Friday."

I'd forgotten about that. "If I fail it, I'm off the team."

"Well, we'll have to make sure you don't fail it, then, won't we?"

Yeah, fat chance of that.

"Hey!"

I looked at him. "What?"

"You're getting it. Can't you tell the difference?"

"No."

"Yes, you can." He grabbed the homework I'd started before he got there. "Look. You've already done the first two problems." He peered closer. "And you got them right."

"Really?" I snatched the paper out of his hand. "I did?"

He grinned. "Yep, you did. See?"

I ran my fingertips over the paper, as if I could feel the scribblings. "Maybe." Just maybe some of Matt's brains were rubbing off on me. I hoped so.

"You ready to study?"

I set the paper down. "Yes." And I wasn't going to look at his lips once all night, and there was no way I was going to think about kissing him.

Yeah, right.

* * *

Coach Thompson called me into his office after practice on Tuesday. "Sit down, Natalie."

I flopped into the folding metal chair across from his desk. "What?"

"I want to talk about the race."

"The one I sucked in? What about it?" I cleaned dirt out from under my fingernails and swung my muddy foot. It had been raining today, which meant I was filthy.

"What happened? I don't think I've ever seen you run that badly. Not even last year."

"I ran slow."

He got up, walked around his desk and leaned back on the front edge of it. "Natalie."

His voice was all soft and warm, so I looked up. "Yeah?"

"I'm not blind. Val and her group have ignored you for the past two days. Is that what's bothering you?"

I frowned. "I don't care about them."

"Want me to talk to her about it?"

"No!" I jumped up. How embarrassing would that be? "I'm fine."

"You're not fine, but you need to be. We have another big meet this weekend, and we aren't going to win it without you."

I felt like screaming! Everyone wanted me to run fast so the team could win! Didn't anyone care about me? There was more to me than running!

"Natalie? What's wrong?"

Argh! "Nothing. Fine. I'll run fast. Don't worry about me."

"How's the tutoring going?" There was no way to miss the flicker of worry in his eyes.

Worry that he'd lose a good runner, not worry for me personally.

Whatever.

"It's fine. I have a test on Friday."

I think Coach might have actually paled. "Do you need the rest of the week off from practice to study? That's no problem."

"I think I need the practice, don't you?"

"It doesn't matter how fit you are if you fail that test."

Good point. Although, maybe I *should* fail. That would fix everyone who wanted me to be on the team just so the team could win. Treat me like the plague just because I had a bad day on the course. Hah.

"You want the rest of the week off?"

I shrugged. "I'll see. If I don't show up, you'll know I'm studying. Okay?"

He nodded. "Make sure you pass that test."

"Why?"

Coach blinked. "Because we need you on the team."

"Yeah, that's what I thought." I slammed the door on my way out. What was my problem? Shouldn't I feel happy that everyone wanted me and that I was such a necessary ingredient for success? Probably, but it was putting way too much pressure on me, and I was not digging the blackball treatment because I ran badly.

Maybe I should go back to JV.

"Nat?"

I spun around to see Zach jogging down the hall toward me. He was covered in mud like I was, but he looked totally hot. Unlike me, who hardly looked like a girly girl who would interest a boy. "What do you want?"

"What did Coach want to talk to you about?"

"The fact that I sucked on Sunday." I glared at him. "And don't you dare say one word about it. I'm tired of hearing it." Yeah, being hostile probably wasn't the way to win him over, but I didn't care. I was sick of the whole game.

Zach fell in beside me as we walked back toward the locker rooms, our muddy running shoes making squishing noises on the cement floor. "The offer still stands to double before school."

I shot a glance at him. I'd forgotten about that. "Why do you care how I run?"

He shrugged. "You're on my team. I'm the captain. It's my job to make sure everyone has what they need."

"You're the boys' captain. In case you didn't notice, I'm not a boy."

"I noticed."

There was something in his tone that made my stomach leap. Was it because of the kiss he'd witnessed? I felt my cheeks heat up, and I didn't look at him. How could I? I was totally wigging out.

Zach didn't seem to notice. "You're better than how you ran Sunday." He was quiet for a minute, then he added, "Don't let Val bug you."

I tensed. He'd noticed too? "I'm not."

"She's threatened by you. You'll be beating her by the end of the season if you work hard enough."

I slanted a glance at him. "You think?" I had to admit, I liked the sound of that. Then maybe I'd rule the team and she'd have to be my peon.

"Yep."

Then I thought of what she'd said about him. "Why do you want me to beat Val? Didn't you dump her this summer?" If I was going to be used as a pawn in the Val/Zach fight, I needed to know. Not that I would decline to hop in on Zach's side, but I still wanted to know.

He shrugged. "If you run your best, it helps all of us."

Nice vague answer that told me nothing about his true motivations.

He stopped outside the boys' locker room. "So? Are we on for tomorrow morning? Six-thirty on the field?"

I hesitated. I didn't know what I wanted.

"You want to beat Val?"

Yeah, I did. I really did.

He grinned at the look on my face. "Then I'll see you in the morning. You need a ride?"

"Um . . . I guess." I mean my mom could probably drive me, but . . .

"Great. I'll pick you up at six-fifteen. Come dressed to run because we have to be going by six-thirty."

Because a normal girl would take too long to change out of street clothes. Hadn't we already established I wasn't a normal girl?

He disappeared into the locker room before I had a

chance to accept his offer, not that I needed to. He'd taken the answer he wanted and left. I'd have to track him down if I wanted to back out.

I wasn't in the mood to track down any guys, so I guessed I was going to be waiting for him at six-fifteen tomorrow morning.

Taking a deep breath, I shoved my hip against the girls' locker room door and headed inside to the lair of the deadly Queen Val. With any luck, the whole lot of them would have drowned in the shower.

10

We were all assembled at the mall at eleven Saturday morning, drinking lattes at Starbucks before the girls' day kicked in. All my friends were there—even Frances had decided that Theo would survive if she skipped one game. They were there for the single purpose of turning me into a girl, and I was no longer in the mood.

Allie laid a sheet of paper on the table. "So, this is my plan for the day. First, haircut and color. Your appointment is at eleven-thirty. Then off to Bloomies for a makeover. Then we'll do some serious clothes shopping." She frowned. "Or maybe the makeover should be last so you don't get makeup all over the clothes." She scribbled on the sheet. "We'll change the order. I'll stop in at Bloomies to reschedule your appointment. So clothes is second. You need sexy lingerie and some hot outfits for school as well as some date outfits and . . ."

I held up my hand. "Let's skip it."

Allie's head snapped up and she stared at me. "Skip what?"

"All this. How about we go rent a bunch of movies

and eat popcorn or something?" I looked at Blue and Frances. "You guys game?"

I shifted under three hostile stares.

"Let me get this straight," Frances said. "I skipped Theo's game for no reason? Is that what you're saying?"

I glared at her. "If you think hanging out with me and the rest of your friends is 'no reason,' then yeah, I guess so." I widened my circle so my glare encompassed all of them. "Is that what all of you think? That I'm a waste of time because you all have boyfriends you'd rather be with? Because that's the sense I'm getting. Let me know now, and I'll save all of you the effort of having to avoid me."

Allie looked shocked, but Blue and Frances wouldn't meet my gaze.

I hated them. Right then, I knew that I hated them.

Allie touched my hand. "No way, Nat. You're wrong. I'm happy to hang out with you."

"Is that why you all have been having your triple dates and I didn't get invited until I had someone to bring?"

"Ah . . ." Allie shifted and looked at Blue and Frances, who both seemed suddenly interested in inspecting their lattes. "That had nothing to do with you. It just . . . well . . . it would have been awkward to have you there. I mean, because we were all couples and stuff."

"Is that right? How come it was okay when Colin and Theo hung with the four of us when you and I didn't have boyfriends? And suddenly, when there's only one left, it becomes awkward?" My hands started shaking so I shoved them under the table.

Frances finally looked up. "Well, it doesn't matter anyway, does it? Because you have a boyfriend."

"Yeah," Blue chimed in. "We're going out Friday night. Are you and Matt in?"

I stared at them in disbelief. "That's it? It's all okay because you think I have a boyfriend?"

"We *think* . . . ?" Allie frowned. "Don't you?"

"I made it up!" I was so angry I couldn't even think. "I made it up because it was the only way I could hang with my own friends who have been my best friends since I was three years old!"

They all looked shocked. "You made it up?" Blue asked. "He's not your boyfriend?"

"No, he's not!" I wasn't going to tell them the truth, though. "And if you tell my parents that, I will never, ever forgive you!"

Allie looked confused. "You *want* your parents to think he's your boyfriend? Why?"

"Yeah, usually it's the other way." Frances laughed. "Remember? I told my parents I was tutoring Theo? That really pissed him off. He was so offended that anyone would believe he was dumb enough to need a tutor."

Tutoring Theo? I tensed. Too close to the truth.

"Are you okay? You look like you're going to pass out." Blue peered at me.

"No, I'm not okay. I hate all of you." I folded my arms across my chest.

Blue narrowed her eyes and leaned forward. "Tutor."

I jerked.

"Tutor."

"Shut up."

"Why didn't you want us to know he's your tutor?"

"Shut up!" I threw my napkin at her, but she batted it away. "He's not my tutor! I'm not stupid!"

Frances was looking at me with sympathy, and Allie was still sporting a confused look. "Of course you're not stupid," Frances said. "Having a tutor doesn't mean that."

"Said by the girl who gets straight As in everything."

"I'm telling the truth." She frowned. "Why didn't you tell us?"

"Because none of you are my friends anymore! The only way to get your attention was to have a boyfriend." I wiped my sleeve across my face, clearing off the couple of tears that had escaped. "I hate all of you." But I couldn't muster up the same amount of venom as before. I was exhausted. Drained. "I really hate you."

While I tried to catch my breath, the rest of the table sat in silence. Good. I hoped they were all miserable.

"I'm sorry," Blue said. "I had no idea."

"Because you're too infatuated with your college boyfriend," I spat out.

"I know."

The soft tone of her voice caught my attention, and I looked at her. "Really?"

She nodded. "I'm sorry."

"Me too," Frances said. "Why didn't you say anything?"

"Why should I have to? You're my friends. I shouldn't have to beg for attention." I shook my head. "Do you guys even care how miserable my life is right now?"

"Yes!" It was a three-way outburst, and I almost smiled at their response.

"Tell us." Allie retrieved four muffins from the counter and set them on the table. "My treat. Fill us in."

I picked up the chocolate one. "I don't want to waste your time." Yeah, I sounded whiny and pouty. So what? I deserved to be a little high-maintenance for once.

Blue kicked me under the table. "Shut up. You're not. Spill. None of us is going anywhere." She looked at Frances and Allie. "Are we?"

"Heck no," Frances said. "Talk."

"Yeah." Allie propped her chin up on her hands. "What's going on?"

I looked around the table at the faces of my three friends, and for the first time in ages, I felt connected. Truly connected. "You really want to know?"

The expressions on their faces gave me the answer I wanted.

They cared. Sure, they'd been blowing me off lately because of their boyfriends, but they were my best friends, no matter what. They wouldn't disown me if I ran slow or got a bad grade. I could tell them anything. And I was going to, because I needed them. "It started with Ms. Olsen trying to get me kicked off the team."

That statement got an appropriate round of horrified gasps, and I grinned. It was so good to have them back.

"So, I've spent this week training with Zach in the mornings, and studying with Matt at night, and neither of them has so much as hinted at any interest in me. Zach's all about running, and Matt's just into the geometry." I leaned back and took a bite of my third muffin. Allie had been keeping us supplied, and it had taken me almost an hour to get everyone up to speed.

"How did the test go?"

Typical Frances. Nothing was more important than school and grades. "I think it actually went pretty well, but I won't know until next week." I crossed my fingers under the table for good luck. "I hope it takes Ms. Olsen a while to correct them." Oh, please. As much as I'd pretend otherwise, I couldn't bear to be kicked off the team. It was my entire identity, even if everyone hated me. Maybe I could guilt my friends into storming her office and burning all the test papers before she had a chance to grade them.

Frances nodded. "I bet you did fine."

Wish I felt as confident as she did.

Allie waved her hand. "Let's get to the more important stuff. Matt. I think he totally digs you."

I rolled my eyes. "Didn't you hear me tell you what he said about his girlfriend? He's going to go visit her."

"It's a front. He's confused. Kiss him again and he'll realize what he wants."

My stomach flipped at the thought of kissing him

again, and Allie whooped. "Look at her face. She totally likes him!"

"No, I don't." I took a swig of my lukewarm latte. "I like Zach."

Allie's face darkened. "Zach's a jerk."

"Is he the one who stopped by the table on Saturday night?" Frances asked. At my nod, she added, "He's totally cute."

"He's a jerk," Allie repeated. "Don't let him fool you."

"Why is he a jerk?" Blue asked. "I thought he was cute too, and he's been helping Natalie train all week for the meet this weekend. That doesn't sound jerky."

"He was flirting with her in front of Matt. He totally dissed Matt. No respect at all." Allie glared at me. "Given how much you like Matt, you should be totally offended on his behalf."

"I don't like Matt! Not in that way." Heaven help me if I did. He was taken, remember? "Zach was flirting with me because he likes me." I frowned. "Or I thought he did. Doesn't really seem like it anymore." I frayed the edge of my napkin. "Did I tell you about Val?"

Allie snorted. "I can't stand Val."

Blue and Frances looked confused. "Who is Val?"

I filled them in on the Val/Elaine/Zach mess, and by the time I finished, all of my friends were frowning.

"I don't like this Val being all chummy with you," Blue said. "Don't trust her."

"Yeah, pretending she's your friend? I don't believe it." Frances appeared annoyed.

"She has the hots for Zach and she's using you," Allie added. "And don't trust Elaine either."

"Yeah," Frances echoed, and Blue nodded her agreement.

And I started to laugh. "You guys are jealous. Because I might have other girlfriends than you." Oh my gosh. How cool was that? It was awesome.

Rapid denial followed, but they were totally lying.

How good did it feel to be wanted by them? Maybe now they wouldn't take me for granted. "I don't know. Val seems awfully genuine." Except when she's turning her back on me when I walk into the locker room, but no need to tell them that. "And I think Elaine might really be legit. She really isn't a good runner, so she might have issues with Val."

My friends erupted into a frenzied dissertation on why Elaine and Val were alien creatures with evil designs on me and my social life. I was laughing by the time they finished. Until I started to think about what they were saying and realized they might be right. "So what do I do then? I don't know who's telling the truth."

"Date Matt," Allie said. "You know he's legit."

"Matt has a girlfriend." For the millionth time.

"Who lives in London. Come on, do you really think she can compete with you?"

"He's ashamed of me. He doesn't even want me to meet his friends," I pointed out. That still hurt.

Allie shrugged. "So he still has some jock/brain hang-ups. Big deal. He got over them pretty fast when he kissed you." A devious look spread over her face. "That's it! He kissed you because he was jealous of the attention Zach was giving you. It made him realize he wanted you too." She was beaming now. "Definitely get Zach to like you. It'll make Matt come running."

I slammed my fist into the table. "I don't like Matt!"

"She definitely likes him," Blue said.

Frances nodded. "Totally."

"Told you." Allie shot me a smug look.

"Listen." I glared at all of them. "Matt has a girl-friend. They are in love. If I decide I like him, it will suck for me. End of story. If you are my friends, you won't encourage me to do something that's going to make me miserable. Got it?"

Allie stuck her lower lip out in a pout. "I still think he's the one for you."

"It doesn't matter! Don't you see?" How much more obvious did it get?

Frances nodded slowly. "I think you might be jump-ing ship too soon, but I understand. If you like Zach, then I think you should go for it."

"Zach's a total cutie, and he's helping you train." Blue shrugged. "It doesn't matter to me who you go for, as long as you don't start trusting Valerie and her friends."

A disobedient grin crept across my face. So I enjoyed making my friends jealous. So what? They deserved it. Then I frowned. "But Zach doesn't see me as a girl." I dropped my forehead to the tabletop and closed my eyes with a moan of despair. "Why does every guy see me only as a buddy?"

"Matt doesn't," Allie said.

"Shut up! Just shut up about Matt!" When would she give up? As if it wasn't hard enough not to think about that kiss without Allie trying to shove him down my throat. "I'll say this once more, and then if you bring up his name again, I'll disown you. Matt has a girlfriend who he loves, and even if he didn't, he's ashamed of me. End of story."

"I thought Tad didn't like me, but he did."

"Argh!" I jumped up from the table. "I'm leaving."

Blue grabbed my wrist before I could get away and she hauled me back to my seat. "No, we support the Zach thing, and we'll help you." She gave Allie a long look. "Okay?"

Allie shrugged and folded her arms across her chest. "Fine."

Blue picked up Allie's notepad. "Okay, so we missed her haircut and color appointment. I'll reschedule." She pulled out her cell phone and dialed while I pouted and glared at Allie, who squinted her eyes and scowled back at me.

"They have an opening in ten minutes," Blue announced. "Allie, you stop at Bloomies and reschedule her makeover, and meet us at the haircut place."

Allie eyed the rest of us with a sullen look on her face. "I'll help, but it's not to attract Zach. When Matt sees how she looks and notices Zach's interest, he won't be able to keep himself away." She held up her hand at my protest. "Natalie, I owe you for getting me together with Tad, and I *will* repay my debt. It won't be by hooking you up with Zach. You're too good of a friend." She left before any of us could respond.

"I think Zach's cute," Frances said.

"He is." And he was helping me with cross country. "Besides, if Val was right that he was trying to take advantage of me, then I'd hardly have to be battling to get him to notice me as a girl, right?"

Blue's face darkened. "Val's a liar. I can feel it. She wants Zach for herself and she's trying to screw you to get him."

"I agree," Frances said. "Never trust an ex-girlfriend."

I felt my shoulders relax. That was what I wanted to hear. "You think there's any chance of getting Zach *and* not having Val hate me?"

"Why do you care if Val hates you?"

"Because running is my life and she can make it miserable for me if she gets the entire girls' team to hate me." I'd skipped practice this week in order to study after school. Since I was running with Zach in the mornings, I'd figured it was fine. The truth? I didn't want to be at practice and be humiliated and ignored by Val and her friends.

"If you snare Zach and kick butt this weekend, all those girls will come to you and Val will be stuck alone," Blue said.

"You think?"

Frances nodded. "Definitely. You'll be the new Queen of Running at Mapleville High."

Sweet. My first action as queen would be to behead Val.

Blue stood up. "Appointment in five minutes. Let's go start creating the new Natalie."

New Natalie? I *really* hoped this turned out okay. What if they created a freak?

Five hours later, Blue hollered for me. "Natalie! Come on! Our table is ready!"

No way could I drag myself away from the bathroom mirror. I couldn't believe it was me. Me! With golden highlights in my normally drab brown hair that now curved softly around my face instead of hanging wildly or yanked into pigtails. With makeup that made my eyes look huge and gave me cheekbones. Wearing a shirt that made me look like I had a figure instead of a toothpick body. Jeans that hugged in the right places and curved way below my belly button, taking advantage of my cropped shirt. Sandals that showed off my pedicure. Earrings that swung softly against the sides of my neck.

I looked awesome, and I couldn't believe it.

"Nat!" Blue stuck her head in the bathroom. "Come on!

"Is he here?" We'd come to the same pasta place as last Saturday, hoping that it was a team tradition for Zach to come there before each meet and do his carbo loading.

"I haven't seen him, but a red Jeep just pulled into the end of the parking lot, so maybe that's him."

OMG. My heart fluttered and I clenched the edges of

the sink. Was he really here? To see me in my hot new look? "Should I tell him I broke up with Matt?"

Blue narrowed her eyes. "I'm not sure. According to Allie, he's interested because you're unavailable. I think I'd wait."

"Too many games. Ugh."

She grinned. "It's all worth it if he's the right guy."

"I hope." I pushed back from the sink. "Okay. I'm ready."

I followed her out of the bathroom, crossing my fingers behind my back that Zach would be out there in the lobby.

11

No Zach in the crowded foyer.

Deflation whooshed through me. I really wanted Zach to be there. I needed him to be there. After Matt's rejection, I needed someone to notice me as a girl. And Zach had been so nice to me all week. Truly, he couldn't be a jerk.

Allie and Frances were standing by the hostess desk, giving me impatient looks.

"Sorry," I said. "I . . ." A hand touched my arm and I spun around.

Zach grinned at me. "We meet again."

He was wearing jeans and a T-shirt and sneakers, and he looked so cute I thought I'd die. "Hi." Nice strangled voice, Natalie.

His eyes widened, and he gave me a thorough once-over. "You look cute. Different."

I flipped my new hairdo. "So you're saying I didn't look cute before?" It was amazing that I could give him attitude when all I wanted to do was drop on the floor and thank him for noticing. How pathetic was I? Totally.

"No." He checked me out again, and my cheeks got hot. "You look . . . I mean . . . wow."

I felt one of my friends elbow me in the back, and I grinned. "Thanks."

He'd noticed I was a girl! No doubt about that!

"You here with your boyfriend?" He tore his eyes off me and glanced over my shoulder.

"Girls' night out." To tell or not to tell. That was the question.

He looked behind him, and I saw Val and some other members of the team clustered in the corner. Val was here? Total bummer. "So, you want to sit with us then?"

"No, thanks." I nodded at Val. "She hates me, and I don't need to deal with that the night before the race."

Zach frowned. "Did she mess with you before the race last weekend?"

"You could say that." I felt someone step on my heel, and realized I'd revealed too much. "Not that she can bother me or anything, but I don't want to deal with her."

He shifted. "I'll blow off my friends if you blow off yours."

I tensed. "What?"

"You and me. Table for two." He lifted a brow. "What do you say?"

"Um . . ." Should I say yes? Would that be too easy? Or no?

Allie stepped up and put her arm around me. "She'll eat with you. Give her a good pep talk for tomorrow."

I jerked around and looked at Allie. "What are you doing?" I whispered. Since when did she want me to cozy up with Zach?

She nodded toward the doorway, and I looked. There was Matt, standing in the doorway, watching me.

My heart lurched. Matt was here? Why? Not because he thought maybe this was my hangout the night before a meet?

Impossible. Total fluke.

I swallowed hard.

"Natalie? You there?" Zach waved his hand in front of my face.

"Yeah." I focused on him, trying not to see Matt in the background. Who was he here with? His friends? Was his girlfriend in town visiting? "I guess I'll eat with you."

"Gee, make me feel wanted." Zach put on a hurt face and tried to look pathetic. Didn't work.

"You can have our table," Allie said. "We'll wait for the next one."

Blue and Frances were standing back, grinning their heads off. Why not? All the work we'd put in today was paying off, wasn't it? Zach was here, and he was practically drooling. Everything I'd wanted.

"Thanks." Zach tucked his hand around my elbow and guided me up to the hostess, who smiled and led us back into the restaurant.

And all I could think about was Matt in the lobby. Until I sat down across from Zach and looked into those gorgeous brown eyes. Zach was a senior, and he was hot and he was popular and he'd ditched Val to be with me.

"You look really cute," he said.

I grinned and got a warm gooey feeling in my belly. "Thanks."

"I didn't realize . . ."

"Realize what?" That I was a girl?

He shook his head. "Nothing. So what's with the boyfriend? You guys still together?"

I narrowed my eyes. "Why do you care?"

"I don't." He picked up one of my hands and traced the lines of my palm. "Doesn't matter to me at all. I get what I want anyway."

Resisting the urge to pull my hand away, I said, "What do you want?"

"Guess."

"You want a girl who already has a boyfriend so you can say you won?" I had to know. Not that I really expected him to tell me, but I couldn't pretend it wasn't out there. "Or a conquest?"

He frowned. "What are you talking about?"

I pulled my hand away and clenched it in my lap. "Val told me that you wanted to use me and dump me. It's what you do."

He muttered something under his breath that wasn't complimentary, then he shot me a tense smile. "Val and I have a past. We went out for a while, and the breakup was . . . well . . . ugly. She's pretty spiteful and doesn't want me to find anyone else."

"If it's that bad, then why do you go out to dinner

with her and invite her to your parties?" Where were all these questions coming from? Shouldn't I just be basking in the glow of Zach's attention?

Zach shrugged. "We're on the same team. I can't avoid her, can I?"

"Well, no, but going out to dinner with her doesn't seem . . ."

"It's not *with her.* It's with the team and she comes along. And I'm not with her now, am I?"

"No."

"Natalie." I looked up to find Matt looming over the table. I couldn't see his eyes because his glasses were reflecting, but his jaw was tense. "May I have a word with you?"

Zach grinned and leaned back in his chair, clasping his hands behind his head. "She's with me tonight."

He looked like he was taking a little too much pleasure in that fact, and I saw Matt's jaw grind. I almost felt bad for Matt, until I remembered that he was the one with the girlfriend. He was the one who was too embarrassed about me to introduce his stupid fake girlfriend to his friends. Zach was the one who'd ditched his friends to be with me, in public. "What do you want?"

"A word in private." He glared at Zach. "It's important."

"Fine." I dropped my napkin on the table. "Sorry, Zach. I'll be back in a sec."

"No problem. I'll be here." Did he look like he was enjoying himself or what? Big time.

I followed Matt to the corner of the room, where he stopped and faced me. "What are you doing?"

"Eating dinner. What about you?"

He scowled. "That guy's a jerk. Why are you with him?"

"Because he asked me."

Matt blinked. "What?"

"He asked me to eat with him. So I did."

"That's your standard? Date anyone who asks?"

"It's not a date. It's dinner. With a team member."

He gestured to my outfit. "Dressed like that? Not a chance."

Insulting my beautiful new look? "What's wrong with my appearance?"

"Nothing. It's . . . well . . ."

"What?" My voice was crawling with disdain.

"You look like you're trying to impress him."

I lifted my chin. "Maybe I am. He seems to like it."

"Of course he does." Matt looked even more annoyed. "Half your body is hanging out of that shirt."

Resisting the urge to cover my stomach, I glared at him. "I take it Liz would never show a little skin in public?"

He narrowed his eyes. "No, she wouldn't."

"And she's probably smart too, isn't she?"

"Yeah."

"Well, then, I guess we've established two things. One, I'm not Liz. Two, I'm not right for you. A dumb slut. No wonder you're too ashamed of me to introduce me to your friends."

Matt gaped. "I'm not ashamed of you!"

"Hah! You ignore me in class, you ditched me at the last second when we were supposed to hang with your friends. You may think that athletes are the snobs, but you're the real one." I jerked my head in the direction of Zach. "Zach is far less of snob than you are."

"You think Zach's better than me?"

"He's not ashamed of me, and to me that ranks pretty high."

Matt's face was red and his jaw was so tense I thought he'd crack his teeth. "Come here." He grabbed my hand and hauled me across the room. At the last minute, I saw a table full of Matt's friends, guys I'd noticed sitting in the front rows of my classes, but I had no idea what their names were. We stopped in front of the table, and Matt slammed his arm around my shoulder. "This is the girl you all have been wanting to meet. My girlfriend, Natalie Page." He nodded at the table. "Nat, this is Richie, Eric, Steve and Lenny."

Their mouths all dropped open, and more than one set of eyes checked out my bare stomach.

"She's having dinner with her team captain, but she wanted to meet you guys."

I waved vaguely. "Hi."

Matt dropped his arm from my shoulder and turned me to face him. "Before you go back to him, I want you to think of this." And then he kissed me. Hard, fast and short.

What was with all this public kissing? My knees were going to give out on me one of these times and I'd crack my head on a table and land in a plate of tomato sauce.

His friends all grinned and gave a couple catcalls, and my cheeks felt like they were going to explode with heat. "You are a jerk, Matt Turner." I glared at him, then stalked back toward my table.

Matt caught my arm before I was halfway there, but not before I saw Zach watching us intently, looking a little less smug. "I'm the jerk?" Matt spun me toward him. "Me? Why?"

"Why?" I shoved him in the chest. Hard. "Because you're the one who kisses me out of ego. It's only when Zach's around, because you hate Zach and you want to show him you have something he wants. You're the one using me, and I'm sick of it." I shoved him again. "You have a girlfriend, and yet you want me too, as some token piece to show you can beat out the jock if you want to? Well, forget it. I'm sick of being used by you. As of now, we're officially broken up and I don't want you ever kissing me again!"

I left him standing in the middle of the restaurant, looking shocked, angry and embarrassed.

Good.

It wasn't until I sat down across from Zach that I realized what had happened. I started trembling and tears came up in my eyes. It was all true. Matt hadn't ever liked me. He'd merely used me to piss off Zach. His one and only chance to prove to a jock that he was as good as any of them.

I was so stupid. Stupid, stupid, stupid!

"Natalie? You okay?" Zach asked.

"No." I blew my nose in my napkin and wiped under my eyes. So much for my beautiful makeover.

"Did you . . . um . . . just break up with him?"

I nodded. "Don't worry. I know you're only interested in me because I was unavailable. I'm not expecting anything, and to be honest, I don't want it. I'm sick of being in the middle of everyone who has agendas." I set my napkin back in my lap. "Let's eat and talk about running, okay? Forget about everything."

Though the temptation to look over my shoulder and see what Matt was doing was almost overwhelming, I didn't. No way. He wasn't worth it.

"Can't do it."

I sighed and picked at my salad, which had arrived during my public embarrassment. "Can't do what?"

"Forget everything."

I gave Zach an exasperated look. "What are you talking about?"

"I still want you."

I blinked. "What?"

"You're cute, you're funny and you're a great runner. I didn't care about your boyfriend before, and I don't care now. As I said earlier, I get what I want. And I want you."

Resisting the urge to pass out from shock, I studied him. Intensely. Tried to stare past his cute eyes and nice smile to what was hidden beneath. "How do I know I can trust you? I've been hearing a lot of bad stuff about you, and frankly, I'm not interested in getting involved with a jerk."

"Trust me, how?"

"That you're not lying to me."

He shrugged. "I'm not. I want you and I'll get you."

Aside from the arrogance that deserved a kick in the shin, he hadn't answered the question I'd meant to ask. "I mean, how do I know you won't jerk me around like Val said?"

"If I was that bad, would Val want me back?"

I frowned. "Does she want you back?"

"Of course. Why do you think she's giving us evil glares?" He gestured to his right, but I didn't look. Why bother? I already knew what her evil glare looked like.

I was so confused I felt like my head was going to explode.

Zach reached across the table and set his hand over mine. "We'll take it slow, okay?"

I stared at our entwined hands. Why wasn't my body going all zingy the way it did when Matt kissed me? Probably because I was still upset over the "breakup." It's not every day a girl breaks up with a guy who she isn't even dating. "Okay."

Zach grinned. "How about a real date next Friday night? You and me. The real thing?"

I forced a smile. "Yeah. That would be cool."

"Good." He rubbed his thumb over the back of my hand. "Wear this outfit again. I like it."

Victory.

Sigh.

12

I was doing strides to warm up for the race when Val stepped in front of me. I tried to dodge her and keep running, but she grabbed my arm. I tried to shake her off. "Val, I need to get ready. Leave me alone."

"What's going on with you and Zach?"

I stopped struggling. "Maybe I should ask *you* what's going on with *you* and Zach?"

"What do you mean?"

"He says he dumped you and you want him back, so you're trying to sabotage any relationship he has. You say he's a jerk and you're trying to protect me from him. Who's lying, Val?" I pulled away.

She paled. "He said that?"

"Yes." The beauty of already being soundly rejected by the cool kids was that I didn't have to worry about messing up my chances with them. I had no chance, so why bother to put up with her attitude? She might hate me, but she'd never take away the fact that I could run.

Actually, she'd done just that last weekend, but I wasn't going to let her do it again. "We can talk after the race. I need to get ready." I sprinted off before she could grab me again, then I found a spot away from the others.

I closed my eyes and jogged in place, snapping my knees up to my chest. My tension seeped away, my mind settled in my legs, and the race became my world. When I opened my eyes, I was ready. Clear, settled and focused.

Today was *my* race.

Allie tackled me with a huge hug after the race. Blue fell on top of her, and Frances next. "You are so awesome!" Allie shrieked, while Blue shouted something about victory and Frances chanted my name.

"Get off me, you guys. I can't breathe." But I was laughing. God, was I laughing.

"Did you see Val's face when the results went up and she saw that you'd beaten her at the finish line?" Allie rolled off me onto her back, lying on the grass with her arms up in the air. "That was so awesome!"

"I thought she was going to kill you right then," Frances said. "Theo was ready to rip her off and throw her down if she touched you. Oh my gosh, that was the best moment ever. I can see why sports are addictive."

I sat up and wiped fresh mud off my cheek, courtesy of the friend tackle. "It was cool, wasn't it?"

"Cool?" Blue grabbed my hands and pulled me to my feet so she could give me a giant hug. "It rocked! A double victory! You win, *plus* she loses! Does it get any better than that?"

"Yeah, because you guys were all here to cheer me on!" They were all I needed. I didn't care that Matt wasn't here or that he was a jerk who had used me to try to get back at all the jocks of the world. Wait a sec. I was still furious about that. How dare he use me? Jerk!

"We are so going out tonight to celebrate," Blue announced. "Our treat!"

A heavy male hand came down on my shoulder and I spun around, my heart catching in my throat.

Only Colin, Blue's boyfriend. "Great job, Natalie."

I grinned. "Thanks."

Then Theo showed up and gave me a huge hug. "Frances told me about Val. Forget her." He put his lips next to my ear and lowered his voice. "She hit on every member of the lacrosse team before she started dating Zach. She's a piece of work and I'm glad you beat her." He winked. "She didn't get me, and don't let her get you."

I stared at him as he released me. I'd forgotten that Theo might know her, seeing as how he had graduated from our school only last year. "What about Zach? Do you know him? Is he a good guy?" Theo would know the truth. Guys talked.

His eyes flicked to Frances, who gave him a stern look. He shrugged. "I don't know."

"What? Yes, you do." I threw my hands onto my hips. "Frances! What do you know? Why won't you tell me?"

"All he knows is dumb locker room talk that means nothing," Frances said.

"So? Tell me what you know." I grabbed Theo's arm. "Tell me!"

"He's still in love with Val," Theo blurted out.

I dropped his arm. "What?"

Frances shoved him aside. "Don't listen to him. It's guy talk. They don't know. Really, it's conjecture."

"But why do you think that?" How could he still love Val? I mean, she was a horrid person and he'd been so nice to me.

Theo shrugged. "I don't know. Guys talk. That's the theory."

"See?" Frances slugged him. "It's a theory, and Theo hasn't been at the school since last year. So it means nothing. Last time Theo was around Zach, Val was still dating him, so how does he know what's going on now?"

Allie cleared her throat. "If he's in love with someone else, you better watch it."

"Yeah," Blue added. "You could get hurt."

"Kinda like Matt, huh? Who you guys have been trying to foist on me? Why is it okay for me to like Matt, who we know is in love with someone else, but not okay to like Zach, who we guess might still be in love with a horrid evil creature he couldn't possibly love?"

"Because Matt's wrong and he'll realize that," Allie said. "It's simple."

I shook my head. "You guys are unbelievable. Unbelievable! Why do you like Matt so much?"

Allie sighed. "Because he's honest and he treats his girlfriend fairly. The only person he's lying to is himself, and you can't say the same about Zach, who freely lies to get what he wants. Like telling you the party was for team members only so you wouldn't bring Matt. He's a liar, and it'll burn you."

"If he was that eager to get me there, then how can you say he loves Val?" Besides, the only reason Matt had kissed me was to prove himself to Zach. Sorry, but that wasn't true love. It was the actions of a jerk, who I was *not* going to let break my heart.

"Maybe Zach's trying to make Val jealous by paying attention to you?" Frances suggested.

"But he's the one who broke up with her." So both guys were using me to try to impress someone else? No, I wasn't going to think like that. Yes, it was confirmed with Matt, but I wasn't going to let a bunch of stupid rumors and theories make me think the same of Zach. I needed *someone* to like me for who I was, even if he was a player!

Blue shrugged. "I think you should go for Zach. See how it feels. If it doesn't work, it doesn't work. You move on. The only way I figured out what Heath was like was to go on a date with him. So do it. Just go, have fun and see what happens."

I hugged Blue. "Thank you! That's what I needed to hear!" I looked at everyone else. "I love you guys, but I can't hold out for a boy who's already dating someone else and who uses me to get back at the enemy, which includes all jocks. I'm going on the date with Zach next Friday, and I'm going to have fun."

Allie shrugged. "It's your life. Do whatever you

want. I'm going to head over to watch the boys' race. Tad's in it."

The group decided to join her and I let them wander off.

Then I quietly went to another part of the course to watch Zach.

Zach, who wanted to go out on a date with me. What more could I ask for?

The front pack came into view, and Zach was third. I screamed for him as he went by, and I swear I got a smile from him.

See? I knew what I was doing.

At the end of class on Monday, Ms. Olsen looked at me. "Natalie, can you stay after for a minute?"

Oh, no. She'd graded my test over the weekend. I was going to be sick.

Matt glanced over his shoulder at me and gave me a nod. Yeah, right! Like that would help. It was too late!

I slumped in my chair and waited for everyone to leave. Blue gave me a pat on the shoulder, and I realized that I was glad I'd told my friends about my situation. They didn't think I was stupid, and it helped to have someone who understood.

How was I going to talk my way out of it? Let's see. Matt and I had only been studying for a few weeks. Not enough time. I needed more time. And my homework had been great, right? I mean, sure, he'd been helping me, but I'd been getting some stuff on my own lately. He'd said so himself!

Matt was the last one to leave, and he didn't get up until Ms. Olsen told him to. "This is between Natalie and me."

He shot me a sympathetic look, and hauled his books out of the room, shutting the door behind him.

That was thoughtful. If I was going to have my life destroyed, I definitely wanted the door closed. No need for the world to know. Can you imagine if Val was walking by? She'd probably be so excited she'd post flyers about it.

Ms. Olsen adjusted the glasses on her nose. "I graded your test."

I slid farther down in my chair. "I figured."

"Your homework has been better."

"Yeah." Come on, put me out of my misery and tell me!

"How is it going with Matt?"

"He's a good . . . teacher." I wasn't going to call him a tutor. Not in public.

"Good. I thought he would be."

Yeah, yeah. So Matt was a god. I wasn't in the mood to sing his praises.

Ms. Olsen pushed back her chair, picked up a paper from her desk and walked toward me. It was like the stealthy approach of a rabid panther, stalking me, ready to pounce and rip me to shreds, her fangs being that piece of paper dangling from her claws.

I leaned back in my chair and wished really hard that she'd turn tail and go stalk some other poor unsuspecting student.

But she reached my chair intact and set the test down on my desk.

I refused to look at it.

"You got a B-minus."

Disbelief surged through me and I grabbed my paper. There it was. A big red B-minus on the top of the page. Oh wow.

Wow.

Wow.

Wow.

She smiled and patted my shoulder. "I knew you could do it."

A B-minus. I got a B-minus. I'm so smart. Soooo smart. So supersmart.

"Keep it up, and your spot on the team is safe."

I finally looked at her, totally unable to keep the giant grin off my face. "Thanks."

"You're smart, Natalie. It just took a little guidance. Good job."

Good job. I'd done a good job. Yahoo!!!!!

"Now, get out of here before you're late for your next class."

"Right!" I grabbed my books and nearly skipped out of the room. B-minus! Rock on!

I flung the door open and jumped out into the hall.

"Well?"

I spun around to find Matt leaning against the wall. "Matt!"

"I assume it was about the test. What did you get?" His jaw was a little tense. Worried about his reputation?

Hah! Not with me around to bail him out! "B minus!" I thrust the paper at him. "Look!"

"No way!" He grabbed the test out of my hand, his fingers brushing against mine. Which I totally noticed, of course. He might be a jerk, but it was hard to forget those kisses. He looked up, a huge smile lighting his face. "You're a stud."

I grinned. "A stud?"

"Yeah." Before I knew what he was doing, he grabbed me and gave me a hug. A big, fat hug that smashed me against his chest. A hug that felt so incredibly awesome. After a moment's hesitation, I hugged him back. Not because I liked him or anything, but because we'd gotten that B-minus together, and we deserved a team hug.

After what felt like forever, but not nearly long enough, he let go, and so did I. He was still beaming. "Can I keep the test? I want to look it over."

"Sure."

"I'll bring it by when I come tonight."

I flipped my new hairdo at him. "Maybe I don't need tutoring anymore. After all, I got a B-minus."

The light left his face so fast it was as if a black cloud had whooshed down and crushed him. "Is that what she said? No more tutoring?"

He looked so bummed, I grabbed his arm. "No, she didn't say that. I was kidding. I still need you."

"You sure?"

"Yes!" I nodded at the paper. "I'm not stopping with a B-minus. By the end of the semester, I want an A. Think I can do that on my own?"

A half smile curved one side of his mouth. "An A, huh? I think we can manage that."

"Really?" Hope lit through me. "I was kidding. You think I can get an A?"

"Of course. Look what you've done in a couple weeks."

Wow. "Really? You're not just saying that?" A warm feeling settled in my belly. "I thought you thought I was stupid."

Matt frowned. "Why do you keep saying that? Did I do something to make you think that?"

"Well, you didn't introduce me to your friends. . . ."

"I did. And you got mad at me."

"That was because you kissed me! I mean, not because you kissed me, but because of *why* you kissed me."

He frowned. "Because I was trying to make Zach mad."

"Yeah."

"Is that worse than kissing you to make everyone think we're going out when we're not?"

"Yes!"

"Why?" If he hadn't looked so genuinely confused, I would have kicked him in the shin and told him to go tutor someone else.

"You really don't get it?"

"No!" He sounded exasperated now.

"You two still out here?" Ms. Olsen walked out into the hall. "You better get to class or you're going to be late." Then she smiled. "Nice job, Matt. You two did well."

He muttered a thanks, but he still looked aggravated.

"Go!" Ms. Olsen gave us each a push. "You don't want to end up in detention after a great start to the day."

Matt shot me a look. "I'll see you tonight."

Something in his eyes told me the conversation wasn't finished, and I wasn't sure what I thought about that.

13

My doorbell rang at six-forty-five, fifteen minutes before Matt was supposed to arrive.

I opened it anyway.

He was standing on my doorstep with flowers.

Flowers?

"These are for you." His cheeks were a little pink and he shifted his weight back and forth.

"For what?" Oh my gosh. No one had ever given me flowers before. Had he broken up with his girlfriend? Was he here to tell me he was madly in love with me and he couldn't live without me?

"For the B minus on your test."

My heart fell. "Oh."

Dad stuck his head around the corner. "Flowers for Natalie? What's the occasion?"

Total embarrassment.

Matt grinned at my dad. "She did really well on a math test today. Best grade of the year so far."

"Matt!" That was one step away from confessing the tutor thing!

My dad looked pleased. "Great news, hon." He clapped Matt on the shoulder. "You're a good influence on her. I've never seen her study as regularly as she does with you." He nodded at me. "Keep this guy around, Natalie. He's a good one." He turned away, shouting for my mom, no doubt to tell her the good news, leaving Matt and me in the front hall alone.

Matt held the flowers out. "Don't you want them?"

"Oh, yes. Of course." Flowers were still flowers, even if they weren't about declarations of love, weren't they? I stuck my nose in them and inhaled. "They're wonderful. Thanks. No one's ever given me flowers before."

He shrugged, but looked pleased. "Glad I could be the first."

Was this guy a keeper or what? Totally sucked that he had that girlfriend. And I was still mad about the using-me thing, but the flowers would go a long way toward making me forget about that.

Matt followed me into the kitchen, where I started rifling through cabinets, looking for a vase. "Natalie? Can we . . . um . . . talk for a sec?"

"Yeah, sure." I squatted down and pulled open the cabinet under the sink. "What's up?" No vases.

His hand closed over my arm and he pulled me to my feet so I was standing only inches from him. So near that he could kiss me by barely moving his head. Oh my gosh. Was that what he wanted to talk about?

"I'm sorry about kissing you," he said.

"You are?" Hardly what I'd been hoping to hear.

"You were right. I did it to piss off Zach." He dropped

160

my arm and walked across the kitchen. "I thought it was okay, I guess, since we aren't actually dating or anything."

"Shh!" I checked the door, but no parents were lurking.

"I was wrong. I hurt you, and I feel cruddy about it." He rubbed his chin. "You're a jock, but you're not bad, and you didn't deserve that."

"I'm 'not bad'? What does that mean?" I held up my hand. "You know what? Forget it. You still have jock issues, and I don't want to hear about them. Yeah, sure, you introduced me to your friends, but you still see this jock label hanging over my head."

"Don't you do the same to me with a brain label?"

I shook my head. "No. I judge you as a smart guy who has more attitude than any jock I've ever known." I lifted my chin. "Even Zach."

His face darkened. "That guy's a jerk."

"Yeah, well, get over it. You don't have a right to judge my social life." I finally pulled out a vase and shoved the flowers in it. "I'm going on a date with him on Friday, and that's it."

"Don't."

I spun around. "Hey, Mr. I've Got a Girlfriend! Just because you're hopelessly in love doesn't make you some expert on the dating scene. I like Zach. He's nice to me. He asked me out. Until you ask me out on a real date, you can't say anything!"

He looked shocked. "I have a girlfriend. I can't ask you out on a real date!"

"Yeah, I know." I thudded the vase of flowers on the table. "Shall we study?"

Matt said nothing as he set up his books. I sat down next to him and we silently gathered our papers.

"If I . . . um . . . were to ask you on a date, would you go?"

I looked at him sharply, but he was studying my test intently. Only one raised eyebrow indicated he was waiting for my response.

After taking a minute to catch my breath, I said, "If you asked me, would it be to make Zach or someone else mad? Or for some other agenda?"

His gaze flickered toward me. "Let's say there was no agenda. Would you go?"

"Not if you still had a girlfriend."

He rolled his eyes. "Give me a break, Natalie. Is that what you think of me? That I'd ask you out if I was still going out with my girlfriend?"

"I guess not." He might be a lot of things, but a liar or a cheat wasn't one of them. He was honest and I knew he was one of those trustworthy guys.

"So? Would you go?"

I took a deep breath, then let it out. "Why bother even thinking about it? You have a girlfriend, don't you?"

"Yeah."

"Are you planning to break up with her?" I held my breath.

Matt shook his head. "No."

Damn. Could I feel more bummed? "Then there's no point in discussing it, is there?"

He shrugged.

End of discussion, then.

After a minute, he picked up my test. "I thought we'd go over this. Review the problems you missed."

Back to business. As it should be. Because he had a girlfriend and I had a date with Zach on Friday that I was very excited about.

Zach showed up at my house at exactly eight o'clock on Friday night. My parents had gone to a concert downtown, which is why I'd let Zach pick me up. No need to raise questions about why I was going on a date with another guy when I had a "keeper" already.

He was wearing jeans and a cross-country sweatshirt and running shoes. He smelled good and looked cute. "Hi, Natalie." His eyes swept my outfit, which was another one from our girls' day out. "You look hot."

I grinned. "Thanks." Hot, huh? Never been called that before.

"Your parents here?"

"Nope. You're spared." I grabbed my jacket. "You ready?"

His gaze swept the front hall. "Or we could hang out here."

Alarm whooshed through me. Afraid of being seen with me in public? Aiming to molest me in an empty house? Either way, not good to stay home. "I'm hungry. Let's go out."

"We could order delivery." He stepped inside and shut the door. "Got any DVDs? I'm in the mood to chill." He walked off toward the back of the house without waiting for a reply.

All of Val's warnings started going through my head. "My parents will probably be back soon." I ran after him, shrugging my coat on. "Let's go out."

He was in the family room checking out the DVDs. He held one up. "Let's watch this."

"But . . ."

"What do you want? Pizza okay?" He pulled out his cell phone. "How about a veggie?"

"I'd really like to go out."

Zach lowered the phone. "Are you afraid to be alone with me?"

Yikes! "Of course not." Could he tell I was sort of lying?

"If Val said I was going to attack you, ignore her. She's lying. I won't touch you."

Well, I wasn't sure if *that* was necessary. I mean, a little touching would be okay.

He shoved the phone back into his pocket. "Forget it. Let's go out."

"No." I grabbed his arm. "It's okay. You're right. I was thinking about Val. I trust you." No way was I going to let Val ruin my date.

"You sure?"

"Yes." I took the DVD. "I'll put this in while you order. Veggie is fine."

"Diet Coke?"

"Yeah." I set up the DVD while he ordered, my hands trembling. Not a lot, but a little bit. I sank down in the middle of the couch and wondered where he'd sit.

Zach hung up his phone and eyed the room. "Okay if I sit with you?"

How sweet was that? All the tension went out of me and I nodded. "Yes."

He shrugged off his coat and tossed it on a chair, then lowered himself next to me.

Not touching, but close. Perfect.

"Good job on Sunday," he said.

I nodded. "Thanks."

"Think our training helped?"

"Definitely."

"You could join me again, you know."

I hadn't gone back for the early-morning training this week. My friends and I had decided to keep Zach guessing. He'd gotten a taste of date-Natalie on Saturday night, but then I had to play it cool. Besides, since the test was over, I'd been going to practice, where I'd been subjected to Val's evil glare.

But the other girls on the team were starting to be nice to me anyway, so I didn't care as much about Val. The power of being fast! And the fact that Zach had made a point of chatting with me every day hadn't hurt my rep either.

Davis

"Yeah." Was that noncommittal enough? "Maybe I'll join you in the mornings next week." I hit the play button. "Ready?"

"Sure."

About five minutes into the movie, Zach nudged me. "I give a great foot massage."

Foot massage? That sounded awesome. "Is that an offer?"

"Yep."

Nothing too scary could come of a foot massage, could it? "I accept." I kicked off my shoes.

"Scoot back." Zach pulled my feet onto his lap while I adjusted my position, propping a few pillows against the armrest and leaning back. Oh my gosh. My heart was racing! A foot massage!

Zach pulled a pillow onto his lap and set my feet on it. Then he picked up my left foot and started digging his thumbs into the bottom of it.

"Oh, wow."

He grinned. "Feels good, huh?"

I snuggled down into the pillows. "Like heaven. Where did you learn to do this?"

"Val got plantar fasciitis last season, so I learned how to do foot massage from the athletic trainer. I used to work her feet every night."

Major buzz kill there. "Oh."

"Yeah, she used to love it." He frowned. "I wonder how her feet are. She ran okay on Sunday, though." It was like he was drifting into his own world.

Okay, I wasn't feeling the love right now. "Kiss me."

Zach looked at me sharply. "Seriously?"

"Yes." I wanted him to stop thinking about Val right now. There was a limit to my capacity to be with guys who were in love with other girls, and it was time to take Zach for my own.

He lifted my feet and scooted closer to me, laying my legs across his lap.

My heart started to race and I sat up. He slid his arm behind my back to hold me up and then kissed me.

Boring! What kind of kiss was this? It was like kissing a dead fish.

I tried to move my lips the way Matt had, but Zach barely responded. And I sure wasn't feeling it. It was nothing like any of Matt's kisses. No tingling, no excitement. Just boredom. After a minute, I pushed him away.

He frowned. "What's wrong?"

"I'm not sure."

"Yeah." He leaned back against the couch.

"So, you felt it too?" The utter lack of chemistry?

He sat up. "Let's try again."

"I don't think so." I swung my feet to the ground and stood up. There was no way a guy as cool as Zach was just a bad kisser, so there had to be something else. "You still love her, don't you?"

"Who?" Zach tossed aside the pillow that had been on his lap.

"Val. That's why the kiss sucked. Because you didn't want to kiss me."

Zach frowned. "Of course I want to kiss you." He held out his hand. "Come here and I'll show you."

Stephie Davis

I folded my arms across my chest. "Forget it. You still love her, and that's fine, but don't pull me into the middle of it."

Zach let his arms fall. "I don't love her."

"You sure?" I couldn't get the image of that awful kiss out of my head. I needed a dose of Matt to freshen up.

"She doesn't love me."

"Then why is she making my life miserable? She hates me because you've shown an interest in me!"

Zach frowned, but there was a glimmer of hope in his eyes. "You think?"

"Yes." I couldn't believe Theo had been right. Zach still loved her. No wonder he'd been the perfect gentleman with me. He couldn't bear to touch me.

Ow. Major ego hit.

"I think you should leave."

He stood up and grabbed his jacket. "Yeah, probably." He tossed me twenty dollars. "For the pizza."

"You don't have to . . ."

"I do. I'm sorry." He shrugged on his jacket. "I'll still train with you, if you want. If it helps your running, you should do it."

Honestly, I was getting a little tired of private lessons with guys who were in love with other girls. "Yeah, we'll see."

I walked him to the door. "See ya."

He nodded and walked out.

So much for the makeover. A raging success it wasn't.

14

"Are you bummed about Zach?" Allie asked as we all munched popcorn in her family room.

I'd given them the lowdown on the Zach situation, including the fact that Zach and Val had shown up at practice the next Monday holding hands and looking all gooey. And you know what? I hadn't cared. Not a bit. I shrugged. "No. It was weird, but it didn't bother me at all to see them together." Granted, I wasn't all that high on the smug look Val shot me, like she'd won or something, but whatever. I hated her, so what else was new?

"Then you didn't like him," Blue offered.

"Obviously," Allie said.

"What about Matt?"

I frowned. "What about him?"

"How's it going with him?"

"Fine." If you considered him being Mr. All Business, talking only about math and then bolting as soon as we finished our homework, fine. We hadn't talked about anything but geometry for the last two weeks. "My dad offered him a job next semester because he's such a good influence on me." Matt had gotten exactly what he wanted. There was no reason for him to stick around, and there was no reason to keep the charade up. Oh, God. Was he going to ask Ms. Olsen to assign another tutor to me?

"What's wrong with you? You look like you're going to be sick."

"Nothing." I shoved a handful of popcorn in my mouth and tried to ignore them.

"Is he still dating that girl?" Frances asked.

"I assume so. I haven't asked."

"What about London? Is he still going to visit her over Thanksgiving?"

That was this week. "I don't know."

"Does he know you aren't dating Zach?"

I set down my bowl and glared at my friends. "What's with all the questions?"

Allie eyed me. "Tad thinks he likes you. It was pretty obvious at dinner that night."

"Why? Because he kissed me to piss off Zach?" I shook my head. "It's an anti-jock thing he has."

"Or maybe that's what he wants you to think, because he's got a girlfriend and he feels obligated," Frances said. "Maybe he doesn't want to like you, so he's in denial."

"Shut up." I didn't want to discuss this, because there was a little glimmer of hope inside my belly. "I don't want to talk about it."

"Why don't you invite him to the state meet this

weekend? If he shows up even with all those jocks around, you'll know he likes you," Allie said.

"Yeah, tell him you're not dating Zach," Blue added. "It works."

Frances touched my arm. "Do you like him, Nat? If there was no girlfriend, I mean?"

I sighed. "It doesn't matter."

"Maybe it does," Frances said. "Maybe it does."

I studied Matt while he chewed his pencil, working on our last homework problem for the night. It was a toughie that even he had to think about for a while, which, of course, meant I had no idea. I hadn't bothered to waste brain cells on it, instead thinking about this weekend's state meet.

And okay, so maybe I was also thinking a little bit about what my friends had told me to do.

"You're not working." Matt glared at me.

"Nope. I'm not."

He put down the pencil. "If you don't want to do this tutor thing anymore, that's fine with me."

I blinked. "You want out? Is that what you want?" Oh my gosh. He was really going to walk away, now that he had the job from my dad?

He frowned. "Is that what *you* want?"

No! No! No! I wanted him to sit at my kitchen table every night for the rest of my life.

Oh, God. Had I really just thought that? I wanted Matt? I closed my eyes. I was stupid. So so stupid. How could I be that stupid?

No, it must be residual from the Zach/Val situation. That *had* to be it.

"Natalie? You want to end this thing?"

I opened my eyes. "You got the job with my dad. I guess there's no reason to stick around."

He was quiet before he spoke. "Your state meet is this weekend, right? So the season is over. You got what you want. They can't kick you off the team anymore."

Since when had he kept track of my season? "You know the state meet is this weekend?"

He shrugged. "You got what you wanted, I got what I wanted. I guess that's the end then, huh?"

But . . .

"Timing is good. I'm going to see Liz this weekend, so she'll be glad to know it's over."

I swallowed hard to get rid of the lump in my throat. "You're still going to London?"

He looked at me sharply. "Yes. Why wouldn't I?"

"Well, I don't know. If you weren't going out with her anymore or something, then you wouldn't go. . . ." Sounded lame and pathetic, didn't it?

"But I am."

Yeah, well, you don't have to beat me over the head with it, do you?

He shut his book. "Is that it, then? We call it a wrap? No more tutoring?"

I flattened my hands on the table. "I guess." I mean, there was no reason to continue.

"Okay then." He stood up and slung his backpack

over his shoulder, the kitchen light reflecting off his lenses so I couldn't see his eyes. "I'll see you around."

"Yeah, see ya."

And then he walked out the door, and out of my life.

I stared at the starting line, where I'd be standing in less than a half hour. The state meet was here. Everything I'd been working for ended today.

"Nat?"

I didn't turn around. Val. Just what I needed. "What?" If she started giving me a hard time, I swear I was going to yell at her to shut up, I really was.

She stood next to me, shoulder to shoulder. "Are you nervous?"

"A little."

"We can win, you know."

"I know." There was no hostility in her voice, but I still didn't look at her. "What do you want?"

"Last night, Zach told me that you're the reason he came back to me. You told him I still liked him and that he still had feelings for me. You made him realize it."

I slanted a glance at her. "So?"

"Thanks."

"Seriously?"

"Yeah." No smugness there.

"No problem."

We were quiet, but for the first time, I didn't feel any tension between us.

"Natalie?"

"What?"

"Tonight I'm having the team over to my house, regardless of whether we win or not. I'd like you to come."

"You don't need to invite me."

"I want to. I'm . . . I'm sorry."

Knock me down with a telephone pole. Val was *sorry?* I looked at her, and she shrugged. "I love him. I got a little crazy."

Love. All these girls who loved boys. As if I wanted to hear about that stuff. "It's okay."

She smiled. "You want to warm up with me?"

It was a genuine invite, and I grinned. "Thanks, but I'd rather warm up alone."

"You sure?"

"Yeah." Incredible that I was turning down a chance to warm up with Val, but I didn't care. After being on the receiving end of her taunts all season, I didn't need her anymore. I was fine by myself.

I was, wasn't I? I didn't need Zach or Val. I had my friends, even if they were whacked and a little too interested in their own boys.

"Well, I'll see you at the start, then."

"Yep. Good luck."

She smiled. "Good luck to you. I'll be fighting you for the win."

"I'm sure you will." I watched her jog away, and decided I didn't hate her anymore.

I was still going to try to beat her, though.

* * *

I was holding up the team trophy with Val for the picture when Zach jumped in the frame and gave me a huge hug, after he'd given one to Val first, of course. "Way to go!"

Coach Thompson shouted at Zach to get out of the picture, but he was laughing.

We were all laughing. We'd won! Val had won the meet, and I'd come in third. I'd *really* wanted to beat her. I raced so hard that last hundred yards, but there was no way. She'd simply beat me.

Our team had won, though, which was awesome. First time Mapleville cross country had ever won a state title, girls or boys.

"Way to go, Nat!" I grinned at my parents, who were holding up a "Go, Natalie" poster board. Totally embarrassing. My friends were clustered next to them, all waving their fists while the team stood for the photo.

Or rather, photos. There were about eight photographers, including several for some local newspapers.

We were going to be in the paper! And our photo and trophy would go up in the hall outside the gym, where all the other state champs were displayed.

"Now, a photo with the individual state champ."

That would be Val.

It was a good thing I didn't hate her as much anymore, or it would be *really* hard to swallow her standing up there holding her trophy while all the flashbulbs went off. Zach was standing just off to her right, still cheering and looking so proud.

I folded my arms across my chest and watched. Next

year, that would be me. If I hadn't had to spend all that time studying, maybe I could have run faster. Maybe . . .

"Congrats."

I spun around to find Matt standing behind me. He was wearing jeans and boots and a parka, and he looked so cute. "What are you doing here?"

"Watching cross country."

"But what about London?"

"I'm not there."

Well, duh. "Why not?"

He jerked his head toward Zach. "I saw him hug you."

I started to explain, but then I shut my mouth. If he wanted to think I was taken, good. Protected what little bit there was left of my pride. "Is that why you're here? To fight?"

He shook his head. "No. I told you, I'm here to watch you run."

I frowned. "Really? That's why you came?"

"Yeah." He smiled, a crooked half smile. "I mean, I've already seen you take a test and do homework, so I figured I needed to round it out."

I stared at him. "What are you talking about?"

He glanced around, and I suddenly realized we were still surrounded by a crowd of cheering people. I was surprised my parents hadn't accosted me yet, actually.

"Come here." He took my hand and started walking.

If I had any pride, I would have pulled my hand away and ditched him, but apparently I didn't. Besides, he wasn't in London, was he? I wanted to know why.

Not that I had any hope. Too late for that. But a girl could be curious without being pathetically in love, couldn't she?

Matt dragged me around the concession stand and behind a shed, until we were completely alone. Then he stopped, and dropped my hand. "Now you can't tell me it's because I want to impress anyone. It's for you only."

"What is . . ."

I didn't get a chance to finish because his lips were on mine. I was totally going to die right there. Kissing Matt was just as awesome as before, or maybe even better, because it was slow and sweet and perfect, and his hands were so warm on my cheeks as he cradled my face.

The best kiss in the history of the world.

He pulled back a little and smiled. "I was so afraid I was too late."

"Too late for what?" It was incredible that I could still speak, I was so stunned.

"You." He took my hands and kissed me again. "I broke up with Liz. I never went to London. I couldn't go."

"You're kidding." Yeah, brilliant words of love, but I was too shocked to come up with something poetic. Besides, was poetic really my style?

"Never." He entwined his fingers with mine. "When I left your house and we decided to end the tutoring, and I realized we'd never really hang out . . ." He shrugged. "It was way worse than how I felt when Liz left."

Liz, whom he'd loved?

"But I'm a jock."

"And I made it to your race unscathed. Pretty amazing, huh?"

"But . . ."

"And I want you to meet my friends. All of them. You'll like them." He grinned. "Can you handle dating a brain?"

I finally grinned. A big, goofy grin that I was sure made me look like an idiot. But I couldn't help it. Everything was too perfect. "Dating a brainiac? Well, I never did get the A in math that I wanted. Would you keep studying with me if I dated you?"

"You want to use me for my brain?"

"Yep. Is that okay?" I couldn't keep the smile off my face.

"What if I said I'd tutor you and you didn't have to date me to get my help?" He looked at me intently. "Then what? Still interested in a date?"

How cute was that? He wasn't sure if I wanted him. I draped my arms over his shoulders and clasped my fingers behind his neck. "You have some serious ego problems when it comes to athletes."

His face softened. "I know." He rested his hands on my waist. "Want to help me overcome them?"

I grinned. "I might be willing to help you out, for a kiss or two."

"Deal."

And then he sealed the bargain with his lips.

Stephie Davis

STUDYING BOYS

HOMEWORK: 0
BOYS: 1

So I study. A lot.

So I have a huge crush on the "wrong guy."

Those two little things justify
my friends blackmailing me?
"Meet some other boys or else...."
Hah. What kind of friends are those?

The kind who can get me grounded.

And get me noticed by that "wrong guy,"
who is actually a jerk and no longer my crush.

Or is he?

Dorchester Publishing Co., Inc.
P.O. Box 6640
Wayne, PA 19087-8640

_5382-9
$5.99 US/$7.99 CAN

Name: _____

Address: _____

City: _____ State: _____ Zip: _____

E-mail: _____

I have enclosed $_____ in payment for the checked book(s).

CHECK OUT OUR WEBSITE! www.smoochya.com
_____ _Please send me a free catalog._

Got Fangs?
Katie Maxwell

I used to think all I wanted was to have a normal life. You know, where I could be one of the crowd and blend in, so no one would know just how different I am. But now I'm stuck in the middle of Hungary with my mom, working for a traveling fair with psychics, magicians, and other really weird people, and somehow, blending in with this crowd doesn't look so good.

Fortunately, there's Benedikt. Yeah, he may be a vampire, but he has a motorcycle, and best of all, he doesn't think I'm the least bit freaky. So I'm supposed to redeem his soul—if his kisses are anything to go by, my new life may not be quite as bad as I imagined.

MY ABNORMAL
LIFE
LEE McCLAIN

"But I'm not normal!"

Fifteen-year-old Rose Graham has never been to school. She's never had a date. She certainly never knew she was gorgeous. She's been too busy shoplifting food, keeping Social Services off her family's case, and taking care of her little sister.

Now, plunged into a foster family in affluent Linden Falls, she's supposed to act normal. But everything seems so trivial when all Rose wants is to get her family back together. At least she has the Altlives computer game to help her cope. And Brian Johnson's broad shoulders to drive her crazy....

Didn't want this book to end?

There's more waiting at **www.smoochya.com**:

Win FREE books and makeup!
Read excerpts from other books!
Chat with the authors!
Horoscopes!
Quizzes!